BABOON ROCK

Elizabeth Laird was born in New Zealand but when she was three the family moved to England. Since then she has travelled to the furthest corners of the world and has encountered all kinds of animals. On one adventure she became lost at night in a Kenyan game reserve, coming a little too close to an angry rhino and narrowly avoiding buffalo and elephants. Her experience of the wild animals of Africa has helped her write the *Wild Things* series.

She is the award-winning author of *Red Sky in the Morning*, *Kiss the Dust*, *Secret Friends* (shortlisted for the 1997 Carnegie Medal) and many other children's novels.

Elizabeth Laird has been helped in her research for *Wild Things* by wildlife experts and local people in Kenya, whose lives are constantly touched by the animals amongst which they live.

D1012172

All Wild Things titles can be ordered at your
local bookshop or are available by post from
Book Service by Post (tel: 01624 675137).

WILD THINGS

BABOON ROCK

Elizabeth Laird

MACMILLAN CHILDREN'S BOOKS

Series consultant: Dr Shirley Strum
with the support of Dr David Western,
past director of the Kenya Wildlife Service

First published 1999 by Macmillan Children's Books
a division of Macmillan Publishers Limited
25 Eccleston Place, London SW1W 9NF
Basingstoke and Oxford
www.macmillan.co.uk

Associated companies throughout the world

ISBN 0 330 37149 5

5 7 9 8 6 4

A CIP catalogue record for this book is available from
the British Library.

Phototypeset by Intype London Ltd
Printed and bound in Great Britain by Mackays of Chatham plc, Kent

For Carissa and Guy

*whose mother, Dr Shirley Strum, shared with me
her great knowledge of baboons and introduced
me to some very special ones that she has known
for years and years.*

On the far horizon, a strip of orange light deepened and brightened minute by minute. Dawn was breaking.

Up on a ridge that commanded a view of the rolling hills, clusters of huge boulders, as high as houses, were glowing pink and gold as the first rays of the sun struck them. The baboons, who had spent the night on top of them, huddled together for warmth, began to stir and separate. They looked round, searching for any sign of danger, peering down into the shadows where a hungry leopard might still be lurking. Everything seemed quiet. Dangers had stalked the night but their enemies would be slinking away to their rest now. It would be safe to leave the rocks.

The baby baboon woke with a jerk as his mother brushed a fly off her long elegant nostrils. He scrambled up out of her lap, clinging to her hair with his strong little hands and peered out over her shoulder, alert and curious. His older sister ran up to their mother, her tail flying out behind her. She reached out for her little brother, trying to prise him out of her mother's arms,

I

wanting to play, but she pulled a little too hard and the baby squealed indignantly. His mother had started to move off, but she stopped for a moment at the top of the steepest edge of the boulder to greet her daughter, and they held each other in an affectionate embrace.

The baby struggled out from between them and began to tease his sister, baring his little teeth and chattering, wanting her to play at fighting. She hooked her arm around him and pulled him close to her.

Their mother, satisfied that the baby was in good hands, leaped down from the rocks to greet a friend. Her children began to play, running after each other and squealing, enjoying their game in the glorious freshness of the new morning.

Another young baboon joined the chase. For a moment, the little baboon forgot her brother and ran off after her friend. The baby tried to follow them, but he skidded on the smooth rock and started sliding helplessly towards the edge. He tried to cling on, scrabbling with his leathery little hands for anything to hold on to, screaming with fear.

He was nearly over the edge now, about to fall, to crash down onto the boulders below, where he'd break a leg or arm, or knock himself out with a blow to the head. At the last moment, his sister reached him. Screaming anxiously herself, she grabbed his arm and hauled him back from *the brink. It was just as well she'd heard him today. Tomorrow he might not be so lucky.*

The troop had already begun to move off on their daily expedition to forage for food, the children's mother among them. The young female tucked the infant expertly under her arm and, struggling a little over the steepest parts, she carried him safely down from the rocks to the flat hillside below.

The baby was too heavy for his sister, but he clung tightly to her soft hair and she struggled on gamely with him clinging to her belly. At last they caught up with the rest of the troop and the baby scrambled thankfully into his mother's arms. Safe within their protective circle, he stared out at the world, his deep amber eyes bright with relief.

1

BIRTHDAY PLANS

Afra swung one slim brown leg over the side of the hammock that was slung between two pillars on the verandah, and turned a page of her book. She read the same paragraph twice without taking in a single word, then let the book fall on to her stomach.

I bet there'll be elephants at this weekend place, she thought. Even cheetahs, maybe. I can't wait for tomorrow.

Something nibbled at her leg and she sat up. A goose was pecking gently at her knee with his blunt beak, his bright eyes watching her hopefully.

'Stumpy!' said Afra. 'You made me jump.'

She leant out of the hammock, scooped the goose up into her arms and settled him on her stomach. Stumpy waggled his golden rump and rubbed his neck lovingly on Afra's arm.

'I'm sorry,' said Afra, stroking the down on his chest. 'You can't come with us. But I'll only be away for the weekend and I'll bring you back some of my birthday cake. I promise.'

'Afra!' Sarah's African voice, rich with disapproval, floated out from inside the old bungalow, and a minute later Sarah herself appeared at the verandah door, her ample body wrapped in an apron. She was holding a stained sweatshirt disdainfully between her finger and thumb.

'It was clean only yesterday!' she said. 'And look at the state it's in now.'

'Sorry, Sarah,' said Afra. 'Tom and I were collecting bits of wood to make a kind of shelter for Stumpy, and Tom fell into the stream and I fished him out and then Joseph . . .'

'Joseph!' snorted Sarah. 'That son of mine, always getting himself into places where he shouldn't be. Why I'm letting him go off with you to this place when he should be at home studying, I really don't know! I've a good mind to keep him right here.'

'But you promised!' said Afra indignantly. 'It's my birthday treat! Prof's going to come. I've been looking forward to it for months! It won't be the same without Joseph!' She saw one of Sarah's eyelids drop down slowly in a wink and burst out laughing. 'You're such a tease, Sarah.'

Sarah dropped the sweatshirt on to Afra's dark mop of curls.

'I'm not teasing about this sweatshirt,' she said severely. 'Or about the mess in this house. You come on now, and clear up your bedroom. Miss Tidey will be here by supper time, straight off the

5

plane from America. She is used to everything being nice, I am sure.'

Afra stood up, deposited Stumpy gently on the verandah steps and went into the house. A rustling noise from a corner of the sitting room made her turn her head. Her father was sitting on the ancient sofa turning the page of his journal, his long legs, encased in old corduroy trousers, stretched out in front of him.

'Prof!' said Afra. 'I didn't know you were there.'

Professor Tovey waved his hand at her without lifting his eyes from his journal.

Afra hesitated.

'About Aunt Tidey,' she said. 'What's she like?'

Prof lowered his journal and looked at Afra over his glasses.

'I'm not really sure,' said Prof. 'I haven't seen her myself for years.'

'But you must know,' said Afra. 'You're her brother.'

'Oh, you know what brothers are like,' said Prof, picking up his journal again. 'They never notice their sisters.'

'No, I don't know what brothers are like,' said Afra crossly. 'I don't have any, remember?'

She sat down on the floor beside her father, hugging her knees. She felt a little nervous at the thought of meeting this aunt for the first time in her life.

She mightn't like me, she thought.

Questions were piling up in her head. Aunt Tidey had only ever met her mother a few times, she knew that. Had they liked each other? What did Prof's only sister think about her brother marrying an African? Was that why she'd quarrelled with him? Was that why they hadn't spoken to each other for years and years?

She looked up at him. Light from the windows shone on his glasses and she couldn't see his eyes.

There's no point in trying, she thought. He never answers when I ask him about her. He never talks about my mother.

She felt tears sting the inside of her eyelids and she dropped her head onto her knees.

Sarah came into the room.

'It's nearly four o'clock,' she said. 'Afra, if you're going to meet your auntie at the airport, you'd better get into a clean skirt.'

Afra scrambled to her feet.

'I don't want to go,' she said. 'Prof can go without me.' And she pushed past her father and ran out into the garden.

Afra sat down on a tree stump. Birds were displaying their brilliant green and gold wings overhead and an orange butterfly was hovering over the scarlet flowers of a creeper nearby but she didn't notice any of them. Stumpy came up to her and pecked at her shoe. She bent down absent-mindedly to stroke his silky feathers.

'Why should I bother?' she whispered fiercely.

She looked up. Sounds were coming from next door. She stood up and pushed her way through the bushes to the fence. She peered through it.

'Tom!' she called out. 'Are you there?'

A boy of about the same age stuck his head out of an upstairs window.

'Hang on a minute,' he said, and disappeared.

He came round the side of the house a few seconds later and went up to the fence.

'I've been making your birthday present,' he said, looking pleased with himself.

Afra's scowl lifted.

'What is it?'

'You don't think I'm going to tell you, do you?' said Tom. 'It's a surprise. Where's Joseph?'

'Not back from school yet.'

Afra kicked irritably at the loose earth by the fence.

'What's the matter?' said Tom. 'I thought you were all excited about going off to the country for the weekend?'

'I am,' said Afra. 'Nothing's the matter. It's just . . . oh, I don't know.'

'Just what?'

'My aunt's coming tonight from America.'

Tom looked mystified.

'What's wrong with that?'

'I've never even met her. She's never even been

here before. She and Prof had some kind of fight, years ago. I don't know what she'll be like.'

'I wouldn't mind my Auntie Lynn coming here,' said Tom. 'She's a laugh. And she always gives me loads of presents. I got my skateboard from her last Christmas. I bet your aunt's got presents for you. What's her name?'

'Tidey.'

'Tidey? What sort of a name is that?'

'It's short for Matilda. Prof called her that when they were kids because she was always so neat. It kind of stuck.'

'Tidey by name, Tidey by nature, sort of thing, you mean.' Tom nodded intelligently. 'She sounds a bit of a pain to me.'

'Thanks a lot,' said Afra sarcastically. 'That's really cheered me up.'

'Good,' said Tom, grinning.

A noise above their heads made them look up. A ball of fur had landed on a branch of the mango tree. A long tail hung down from one end of it and a small face with two enormous round eyes protruded from the other.

'Kiksy!' said Afra. 'You're awake early. It's not nearly dark yet.'

The bushbaby launched himself on to Afra's shoulder, caught hold of her ear with one small sticky hand and began to hoot affectionately into it.

'Hey! That tickles!' said Afra, peeling the little

9

creature off her shoulder and cradling him in her arms. She looked up at Tom. 'I'd better go. Sarah's after me to clear up my room before Aunt Tidey gets here. Thought I mightn't get another chance to see you before tomorrow. It's really OK? Your mom and dad are really going to let you come?'

Tom looked back at the bare facade of his house.

'Yes,' he said, 'it's OK, but you should see what mum's making me take. Insect stuff, and a mosquito net, and plasters, and sun cream, and two sunhats in case I lose one of them. She's crazy.'

They looked at each other for a moment.

'She's nice though, really,' said Afra. 'I mean she's your mom, after all. She just hasn't got used to living in Africa, I expect.'

'Yeah, well, maybe your Aunt Neaty or whatever she's called won't be too bad either,' said Tom.

'Maybe,' said Afra. 'It's just that I don't know what to expect. It feels kind of strange, having relatives. Maybe she won't like me. Or maybe I won't like her. Wow, this is going to be some birthday. I mean, do you realize that this is the first time in my whole life that I'm going to have real family with me on the day? Prof never usually makes it, and this time I'll have an aunt as well.'

'Sarah's sort of your family though, isn't she?' said Tom.

'Well, she brought me up, I suppose,' said Afra,

'and she really loves me and all that stuff, but she's got her own family. Joseph and the others. I'm sort of her job.'

Tom bent down to scratch a bite on his leg.

'You will be ready, won't you?' Afra said. 'We're leaving straight after lunch tomorrow.'

2
AUNT TIDEY

Lunch the following day was over and Professor Tovey's Land Rover, parked on the gravel strip at the front of the bungalow, was already half full of boxes and bags.

'Oh dear, I'm sure I should have put that one in the front,' said Aunt Tidey, looking anxiously at the big box she had just loaded into the car. She looked round for her brother. 'Richard? Where is he? Richard! Are you sure we have enough drinking water? I don't feel safe about drinking the local stuff, and I don't like the idea of the children drinking it either. Where's Afra? Oh, there you are! Honey, you should be wearing a hat in the sun.'

Afra stared at her mutinously. Aunt Tidey wasn't at all like she'd expected her to be. She was short and round for one thing, not tall and slim like Prof, and unlike Prof, who wore faded cotton shirts and comfortable baggy trousers all the time, Aunt Tidey dressed in embarrassingly brilliant colours. She was wearing a swirly purple skirt at the moment, and a very pink T-shirt which was stretched a little too tightly across her chest.

A large hat with a red scarf tied round the crown was flopping over her eyes.

Afra turned her eyes away.

'She's only been in Africa five minutes and she thinks she knows all about everything already,' she whispered to Joseph, who was perching on the bonnet of the Land Rover beside her.

'Joseph!' Aunt Tidey called out. 'Run along inside and help Sarah out here with the icebox now, would you? I need to pack it in first.'

Prof wandered out of the house.

'Are you nearly ready?' he said to Aunt Tidey. 'You've got more stuff here than I take on a whole summer's archaeological dig.'

'Oh, you know me, Richard,' said Aunt Tidey, bustling back into the house. 'Better safe than sorry. Ah, here comes Joseph. Isn't the icebox ready yet, dear? I'll go and see if Sarah needs a hand with it. If we don't get it in now, it'll never fit in later.'

She marched into the house. Prof came up to Afra and Joseph and leaned against the car radiator.

'Happy?' he said to Afra, giving her a mock punch on the nose. 'You should be. You'll love it out there. It's fabulous.'

'What's it like?' said Afra.

'It's just a little kind of cottage place,' said Prof. 'Very simple. It was a farmhouse once, in the early days, but the farmer built a big ranch house miles away. He went years ago and no one goes there much any more.'

'Do you think there'll be cheetahs?' said Afra, bouncing with excitement. 'I've never seen one really close up.'

'Might be,' said Prof. 'There were last time I was there. That was years ago, of course.'

'And elephants. You said you saw elephants,' said Afra.

'Yes, we did,' Prof said, smiling at her. 'You'll have a great time. Where's Tom? It's time you were off.'

Afra sat bolt upright, her hands gripping the Land Rover with painful force.

'What? You mean you're not coming? You're not coming too?'

'Oh sweetheart, I'm sorry.' Prof took off his glasses and pressed his thumb and forefinger into the corners of his eyes. 'I can't. I have so much to do. There are exam papers to mark, and something's come up about the conference in Geneva. I just can't get away right now.'

'But you promised,' said Afra, her voice shaking. 'It's going to be my birthday. You've never, ever, been with me on my birthday before and this time you *promised*.'

'You've got your friends, Tom and Joseph,' Prof said, putting his hand on her knee. 'And your aunt. You hardly know her yet. You'll have the chance to get to know each other. You'll get to be good friends. You don't need me.'

Afra swept his hand off her knee.

'I do need you,' she said. Tears were splashing down out of her eyes. 'I need you desperately.'

He put his arm round her resisting shoulders.

'Don't cry, Afra,' he said awkwardly. 'You'll have a good time. I'll be here when you get back on Sunday. You can tell me all about it then. Maybe I'll be able to borrow the institute jeep and get away tomorrow afternoon. I'll try, sweetheart. OK?'

'Hi! Sorry I'm late!'

Everyone turned round. Tom was running in through the Toveys' gate, staggering under the weight of an enormous bag. Joseph slipped off the Land Rover bonnet and went to meet him, and the two boys slapped each other's hands. Then Tom grabbed Joseph by the neck, and Joseph wrestled Tom's arm halfway up his back, and Tom hooked his knee round Joseph's and almost managed to bring him crashing to the ground. They lurched apart and stood grinning at each other.

Afra jumped down off the Land Rover.

'You're not late,' she said. 'You needn't have bothered coming at all. There's no point in going now.' And she ran off into the house.

'What?' said Tom. 'What's up with her?'

Joseph glanced at Professor Tovey, then looked down, embarrassed.

'She thought her daddy was coming with us. But he isn't.'

'Are we really not going?' said Tom.

'Of course you're going,' said Prof, exasperated.

'Who's going to drive the Land Rover then?' said Tom.

Professor Tovey wiped his sleeve across his sweating forehead.

'I asked my assistant from the institute to take you,' he said.

'Kamande?' said Joseph, his eyes lighting up. 'I know him. He used to work with my Uncle Titus at the Kenya Wildlife Service.'

'That's right, he did,' said Prof. 'He knows much more about wildlife than I do. He can drive better too.'

'But Afra would like you to come more than Kamande,' said Joseph softly.

Prof put a hand on each boy's shoulder.

'Look,' he said. 'It's not that easy for me to get away from work right now. You're her friends. She always likes being with you. Make sure she has a good time, OK? Can you do that for me?'

'OK,' said Tom uncomfortably.

'Joseph?'

'Yes Prof,' said Joseph, 'but . . .'

'Here comes Kamande now,' said Prof, looking

over their shoulders at the tall African who was striding through the gate towards them.

'Richard!' called Aunt Tidey from the doorway of the bungalow.

She saw Kamande.

'Oh, it's nice to meet you,' she said, coming up to shake his hand. 'Richard's told me all about you.'

'This is my sister, Tidey,' said Prof. He started to go back to the house. Aunt Tidey ran after him.

'Richard!' she said in a low voice. 'What have you done to upset Afra? She's positively volcanic.'

'I've just told her I can't come with you,' said Prof. 'I suppose I should have explained earlier.'

'You certainly should!' said Aunt Tidey. 'Men! They never think.'

Prof laughed sardonically.

'Oh Tidey,' he said, 'if only you knew.'

Aunt Tidey looked sideways at him.

'You've been thinking about her?'

Prof shut his eyes for a moment. He nodded.

'Afra's birthday's always a difficult day for me,' he said.

Aunt Tidey put her hand on his arm, but he made no response and she let it fall. Neither of them spoke for a moment. Then Aunt Tidey said briskly, 'Well, we can't stay here all day. Either we give the whole thing up and stay home, or else you'd better make your peace with Afra and get her out of the house and into the car. I'm not going to do it.'

'You needn't bother, either of you.' Afra's voice was ice-cold as she stalked up behind them and pushed her way between them. 'No one's going to *get* me into or out of anything. I'll make my own decisions and what's more, I'll keep my promises to my friends, unlike some people.'

She walked to the Land Rover and jumped into the back seat.

'Get in,' she said curtly to Tom and Joseph.

They jumped in beside her. Prof went up and stood beside the car's open window.

'Afra,' he said, 'listen to me.'

Afra wound the window up and turned her face away from him.

'Leave her, Richard,' Aunt Tidey said softly behind him. 'She'll come round.'

She climbed into the front seat of the Land Rover beside Kamande, who was already behind the wheel. 'Oh! I nearly forgot. Where's the big cake tin? We mustn't leave that behind, must we? It has a certain rather important cake inside. I spent the whole of my first morning in Africa making it. Is it there, Richard? Can you see it in the back? Good. Then off we go!'

A frosty silence reigned in the Land Rover as it left the congested streets of Nairobi and began to speed along out on the open road to the north.

Afra hunched her shoulder against the others and looked unseeingly out of the window. There was a knot of misery in her stomach. This glorious weekend, that she had dreamed of for so long, was ruined. She had lain awake night after night, imagining how lovely it was going to be, having her father's attention, telling him things, enjoying his company, with no interruptions from his students or his papers or the telephone. She'd have shown him the bird calls she'd been practising, the rolling hoots of the rainbird and the whistle of the starling, sure that the birds around the ranch would answer her. She and Prof would have gone out looking for animals together, and she'd have amazed him by how much she knew about the different kinds of antelope they'd be sure to see, and how many animal cries in the night she would recognize. Prof would have been different way out in the country, she knew he would. Less distant and careworn. More interested in her.

In the front of the Land Rover, Kamande was politely trying to engage Aunt Tidey in coversation.

'How do you like our Kenya?' he was saying.

'Oh, it's wonderful, really amazing,' said Aunt Tidey, looking over her shoulder at the three silent children in the back seat. 'Any of you kids dehydrated? It's pretty hot in here. You have to keep up your liquid levels in this climate.'

Tom nudged Joseph in the ribs and they smiled

at each other. They each took a swig from the water that Aunt Tidey passed back to them and Joseph offered it to Afra. She took no notice of his outstretched hand and he gave the bottle back to Aunt Tidey.

Tom, sitting by the window on the far side of Afra, ignored the atmosphere in the car and looked out eagerly. He had arrived in Kenya from England only a few months earlier and this was his first trip out into the real countryside. Small fields and little farmhouses covered the hills and the red African earth gleamed between the bright green plants.

Slowly the landscape was changing. The farms became more scattered and rolling open country-side, dotted with flat-topped trees, swept away from both sides of the road. Suddenly, Tom blinked.

'You're not going to believe this,' he announced to the silent car, 'but I think I just saw a giraffe.'

Joseph looked round without much interest.

'Yes,' he said. 'That's a giraffe.'

'But what's it doing?' said Tom. 'It doesn't look like there's a zoo here or anything.'

Joseph looked puzzled.

'A zoo?' he said.

Afra sniffed.

'This is Africa,' she said. 'The animals just live here.'

'What?' said Tom. 'You mean animals like

giraffes and . . . and rhinos and lions just wander about all over the place?'

'Of course they do,' laughed Joseph. 'This is their home.'

'Anyway, zoos are horrible,' said Afra.

'No they aren't,' objected Tom. 'I've been to some brilliant ones in England. In the safari parks it's as if some of the animals are practically free. You have to go round in Land Rovers if you want to look at them. I went to Whipsnade last year with my friend Scott and the monkeys were great. OK, so they were in cages, but they looked happy. One of them spent ages chasing his tail, and then he started chucking nutshells at us.'

Afra shuddered.

'That's so terrible,' she said. 'How would you like to be all on your own in a cage in a foreign country, being looked at all the time with nothing to do but chase your own tail? You'd be miles away from your family and no one would know what kind of place you came from or who your mom and dad were, and they wouldn't care one bit about your feelings.'

She relapsed into silence again.

The sun was already low in the sky when at last the Land Rover turned off the main road and headed down a deeply rutted dirt track. On either side, rough scrubby bushes and trees stretched as far as the eye could see, rolling away into the distance towards the snow covered peak of

Mount Kenya, which was crowned with fluffy clouds.

Kamande pointed up to the right.

'Do you see those big rocks up there, on the hilltop?' he said. 'That is a very nice place for a picnic. You can see many wild animals from there.'

'That'll be fun, won't it, everyone?' said Aunt Tidey, turning round and directing a smile towards Afra. 'We could go there tomorrow.'

Tom was eagerly gazing into the trees beside the road.

'I thought I saw a . . . no, it can't be! Yes! It is! Look, a zebra! Right there! And another, and another – three, six, ten, oh, I can't count them all. They're so amazing. So . . . sort of . . . stripy.'

Everyone laughed and even Afra smiled.

'Zebras have to have stripes,' she said. 'It's part of the job description.'

Kamande looked over his shoulder at Tom.

'You do not have any wild animals in your country?' he said.

'Yes we do,' said Tom. 'Foxes and squirrels and badgers and stuff. There were bears and wolves once, thousands of years ago. We did a project in my primary school about the Romans. They used to go and hunt them.'

'Aren't there any bears and wolves now?' said Joseph.

'No. I suppose they must have all got killed. Hunted out,' said Tom.

Kamande drew in his breath.

'What is it?' said Aunt Tidey, turning to him. 'What did you see?'

'Elephant dung,' said Kamande. 'Look.'

He pointed to the track ahead. Big mounds of dung littered it.

'Elephants! Wow!' breathed Tom, scanning the road ahead. 'I'd love to see elephants.'

Joseph shivered.

'But not too close, please,' he said.

'Why not?' said Tom. 'They're not dangerous, are they? I mean people ride on them and everything.'

'That's Indian elephants,' Afra said, sitting up. 'African elephants are bigger and wilder and more magnificent.'

'They are very dangerous sometimes,' said Joseph. 'They can easily kill a man.' He tapped Kamande on the shoulder. 'Is it fresh, the dung?' he said. 'Do you think they are close?'

'Oh yes,' said Kamande. 'It's fresh. Today. Even this afternoon maybe.'

He leaned over the steering wheel, peering down the track.

'OK, kids. Now I just want to establish a few ground rules here,' said Aunt Tidey. 'When we get to the house, I want you all to stay indoors, right?'

'Indoors?' chorused Tom, Afra and Joseph, looking at each other indignantly.

'Oh don't worry, Mamma,' said Kamande soothingly. 'The ranch house has a fence all around it. It is quite safe to be inside the fence.'

Aunt Tidey had never been called Mamma before, and it flustered her.

'Well, we'll see,' she said uncertainly.

'Even outside the fence the leopards and lions will not come close,' said Kamande, spoiling the effect.

'Leopards?' squeaked Aunt Tidey. 'Lions?'

Joseph created a diversion.

'Look,' he said, pointing ahead to a corrugated iron roof that shone in the evening sun. 'There's the house. We're nearly there.'

3

THE HOUSE IN THE HILLS

The light was going fast when Kamande pulled up outside the long low stone house and switched the engine off, but Afra, Tom and Joseph, jumping out of the Land Rover, could still see how perfect the site was.

The house lay inside a small fenced compound on a gentle slope which rolled down and away, past a reed-fringed pond, into an endless vista of wild hills, which were melting into soft greys and purples now as the light faded. There were some smaller buildings behind the main house, and an old man was hobbling out from one of them.

'*Jambo*,' he said, greeting them in Swahili. 'You are welcome.'

'You must be Julius, the caretaker. Excellent,' said Aunt Tidey, beaming and pumping the old man's hand up and down. 'Is the house open? Do you have the key?'

'You are welcome,' the old man said again without smiling, then he turned to Kamande and began to speak in Swahili, waving his arms expressively.

'What's he saying? What does he want?' said Aunt Tidey.

'He says that unfortunately he has not been informed that visitors are coming today,' Kamande said. 'He does not have permission to open the house for us.'

'What? But this is ridiculous.' Aunt Tidey's warm smile slipped from her face and she suddenly looked quite woebegone. 'Richard expressly told me that everything had been arranged. Tell him, Kamande.'

'I am telling him, Mamma,' said Kamande mildly. 'He is the watchman. He is doing his duty. Please, wait here. Let me go and speak to him some more.'

He took the old man by the arm and gently led him round to the back of the house.

'Well! Really!' Aunt Tidey climbed back into the Land Rover and plumped herself down on to her seat. 'And just when I was so looking forward to a shower and a cup of tea. It's too bad of Richard. He probably forgot to inform them here. It's typical. Absolutely typical.'

Afra frowned at her aunt through the open window of the Land Rover.

'Prof wouldn't have done that,' she said. 'He wouldn't have just sent us all out here without letting them know. He couldn't have done.'

Aunt Tidey took off her hat and shook out her soft mouse-brown hair.

'No, honey,' she sighed. 'I suppose you're right. It must be a mistake. All I know is that I'm hot and tired and thirsty and jet-lagged and there's the supper to get and the beds to make and goodness knows what else. When you get to my age you'll realize that men are simply not to be relied on.'

Afra was opening her mouth to leap to her father's defence when there was the sound of bolts being drawn back from the door of the house. It swung open, and Kamande stood there.

'Everything is all right,' he said. 'There was a letter on the table in the kitchen. It is a little hard for Julius to read, so I read it to him and now he has given us the key.'

'There, you see!' said Afra. 'Prof did arrange it. And you could have relied on Kamande, even though he is a man.'

Aunt Tidey wasn't listening. She had magically revived, had jumped out of the Land Rover and was opening the door at the back of it.

'Where have those two boys got to?' she said cheerfully. 'Tom! Joseph! Come and help unload everything. If I don't get to have some tea soon I won't answer for the consequences.'

Tom and Joseph came running round from the back of the house.

'It's wonderful here!' said Joseph. 'There's a whole herd of waterbuck going down to the pond and—'

'And I saw a mongoose, right here behind the

house,' interrupted Tom. 'At least, I think it was a mongoose. Joseph says it might have been.'

He held out his arms towards Aunt Tidey and she deposited a box in them.

'Take that into the kitchen,' she said. 'Joseph, this one's for you. Afra, here's my bag. Carry it carefully now.'

Afra followed the boys into the house, with Aunt Tidey close on her heels.

'Put the light on, one of you,' Aunt Tidey said. 'It's pitch-dark in here.'

'There are no lights here,' said Kamande's voice from the shadows. 'There is no electricity in this place.'

'What?' Aunt Tidey's voice rose a notch. 'No electricity? Does that mean there's no hot water either?'

'We will make a fire. We will heat some water for you,' said Kamande. 'Julius says there is plenty of wood. He has gone to fetch some for us. Have you unloaded the food yet? Can you give me the matches?'

'Matches? I didn't bring any matches,' said Aunt Tidey. 'I never imagined—'

'Here, I have some,' said Joseph, digging into his pocket.

'And I've got a torch,' said Tom. 'A big one, with spare batteries. Mum was scared I'd tread on snakes and stuff if I got out of bed in the night.'

Afra, who was standing beside Aunt Tidey in the dark, felt her shudder at the mention of snakes, but before she could say anything, Kamande struck a match, and in the few seconds before it went out she could see the outline of the room and its furniture.

'There's a kerosene lamp,' she said. 'Look, on the table.'

She darted over and brought it back to Kamande, who struck another match and lit the lamp. The room was suffused at once with a soft warm light.

It was a comfortable old room. A table with chairs round it stood at one end, and at the other was a battered old sofa and three deep armchairs. There were books on the shelves, and a stack of jigsaw puzzles and games.

'What's that? What is it? Bats!' squealed Aunt Tidey suddenly.

Something small and dark was flitting round the room.

'That's not a bat, it's a bird,' said Afra scornfully. 'Oh, the poor thing. Look, it's lost in here. Can you give me the lamp, Kamande? It'll follow the light outside if we take it to the door.'

Carefully, she carried the lamp outside and put it down on the verandah beside the front door. A second later, the little bird swooped out, banked sharply, showing its perfectly forked fan of a tail, and disappeared under the eaves just above the front door. A loud whirring, cheeping noise from several tiny throats greeted it.

'A swift,' whispered Afra. 'And there's a nest with babies in it.'

She held the lamp up towards the nest. A row of black heads popped out, and four huge beaks gaped hopefully in her direction.

'Sorry, guys,' said Afra. 'I didn't mean to disturb you. You'd better snuggle down now and get some sleep.'

Tom came out of the door.

'We need the lamp,' he said. 'We can't see a thing in here.'

He picked the lamp up and took it inside. Afra sat down in one of the old basketwork chairs that stood on the verandah. She could hear the others inside the house. They all seemed to be talking at once.

'Is this our room?' Tom was saying. 'Hey, Joseph, which bed do you want?'

'I don't mind, Tom. Look, here's another lamp. Wait a minute. I'll get the matches out again.'

'Oh, thank goodness!' Aunt Tidey's voice came from the kitchen. 'A bottled gas stove. Kamande, we must get some water on to boil at once. Did we bring the drinking water in from the car?'

'No need for it here, Mamma,' said Kamande. 'The water here is very pure. It's from a spring.'

'Hmm, well, you can't be too careful. Don't mind me fussing, but I don't want to take any risks. Now where's the other food box? Did the boys bring it in yet?'

Her voice faded as she went out of the kitchen.

They haven't noticed I'm not there, thought Afra. No one cares about me at all. Not one single person in the whole world.

The knot of misery in her chest that had begun to loosen, tightened again.

There was a sound to the left of her and Afra, peering out into the gathering darkness, saw old Julius putting down a pile of wood. He caught sight of the white flash of her T-shirt as she moved and looked towards her.

'*Jambo*, little sister,' he called out to her in Swahili. 'You are sitting there all alone?'

His voice was slow and kind. Afra went up to him. She could speak Swahili nearly as well as Joseph.

'Yes,' she said. 'What are you doing?'

'Making a fire for your hot water,' said Julius, 'and to warm up your hearts too. Later, when you have had your supper, you can sit here beside it with your mother and ask her to tell you stories.'

Afra suddenly felt like crying.

'Afra!'

Aunt Tidey called from inside the house. 'Where are you? Come and help me, honey. We have to get the mosquito nets down before the mosquitoes start coming in.'

Afra swallowed, cleared her throat, and without another word to Julius, ran into the house.

Afra sat silently through supper, pushing around on her plate the sticky pieces of pasta which Aunt Tidey and Kamande had hastily cooked up in the kitchen. She wanted to join in with Tom and Joseph, who kept getting the giggles, especially when Aunt Tidey thought she saw a fly on her plate, and flicked at it with her knife, sending a piece of pasta hurtling across the table. Aunt Tidey had laughed even more loudly than the others, and they'd all looked at her, but Afra's throat was closed and tight and she could hardly swallow, let alone talk.

They cleared the dishes away at last, carrying them into the funny old kitchen, moving the lamp around as they went, so that strange new shadows kept falling on the walls.

'Ooo! Ooo!' hooted Tom. 'I am the ghost of an old dead madman who lived in this house and ate people's toes when they were asleep!'

Joseph doubled over with laughter, and Aunt Tidey poked Tom in the ribs with her plump forefinger.

'You'll be too solid to make a decent ghost, Tom, if you go on eating as much as you did tonight. I never saw anything to beat it.'

Joseph looked out of the window.

'Look,' he said. 'The fire.'

The fire that Julius had lit was dancing merrily now, licking around a large pan that balanced on the stones above it.

'Well, that is nice,' said Aunt Tidey. 'I see that Julius is kindly heating up some water for us. Boys! Afra! Where are you going? You mustn't go outside at night without putting insect repellent on. Come back!'

She was addressing an empty room. Tom, Afra and Joseph were outside already, squatting around the fire. Aunt Tidey hurried after them, a tube of cream in her hand.

'Come on, all of you,' she carolled. 'Put it on. We don't want you going down with malaria, do we?'

The fire was well established now, its red heart glowing brightly.

Julius is right, thought Afra. Fire does warm your heart.

She felt Aunt Tidey rub some cream into her arms. Her hands were unexpectedly gentle, and Afra felt her irritation subside a little. Aunt Tidey seemed to feel the spell of the fire too. She was quiet at last and stood still, gazing down into the flames, one hand still resting lightly on Afra's shoulder. Then Kamande pulled up a log and she sat down on it, resting her chin in her hands.

'Look at the stars,' said Tom into the silence.

They all looked up. The sky was like black

33

velvet stitched all over with a million tiny sequins, while the Milky Way lay faintly across it like a piece of pale muslin. Wood smoke drifted up, glittering with sparks.

In the distance there was a rasping grunt.

'What's that?' said Aunt Tidey anxiously.

'A leop—' began Afra.

'Only a jackal, I'm sure,' Kamande hastily interrupted, giving Afra a conspiratorial look.

Afra grinned at him.

'Tomorrow, if we go to the rocks for a picnic, perhaps we will see some baboons,' Kamande said.

'Oh dear, I heard they can be so tiresome,' said Aunt Tidey, 'thieving from people. The males can be quite aggressive too.'

'Here the baboons are not so used to people,' said Kamande. 'No one has taught them to beg for food, or chased them or frightened them. They are more interested in each other than they are in humans.'

'They're ugly, baboons,' said Tom. 'They've got bare bottoms.' He giggled.

'Oh, that's so pathetic,' Afra burst out. 'That's all people ever say about baboons. But I read a book about them. They're so like us it isn't true. The young ones play like human kids, and they have friends, real friends, and favourite play-mates, and they stick up for each other when there's a fight.'

'I saw a mother baboon with a sick baby once,' said Kamande. 'The baby died in the night. The mother carried it around with her for two days, trying to wake it up. The other baboons came around to help her. At last she seemed to realize that the baby was dead, and she left it.'

'That's very sad,' said Joseph.

'When I was a little kid my rabbit died,' said Tom. 'I cried all night.'

'Prof had a dog once that died, didn't he?' Afra asked Aunt Tidey. 'He told me about it.'

'Oh, that dog!' Aunt Tidey cast up her eyes. 'Richard adored it. Benjy, his name was. He was a darling little spaniel. He followed Richard everywhere. When Benjy died Richard was absolutely inconsolable.'

'Did he never get another dog?' said Tom.

'No. He said it was too painful, loving a dog, and then losing it . . .'

Her voice died away.

From the pond below came a sudden frantic quacking, then, overhead, wings were beating against the sky and a wild mournful honking echoed up through the darkness.

'They're geese, Egyptian geese, like Stumpy!' cried Afra. 'Oh, I hope he's all right.'

Joseph chuckled.

'You reminded Mama so many times about Stumpy and Kiksy I thought she was going to blow up,' he said. 'I don't know why you bothered. She looks after them as well as you do.'

'Yeah, I guess you're right,' said Afra.

Kamande's head was turned towards the pond, and Julius, who had come up with another pile of wood, was standing still, looking in the same direction.

'What's down there?' Kamande asked Julius in Swahili.

'A leopard, maybe. There are elephants around too. Better not say anything to scare Mamma.'

Aunt Tidey was looking at them, unable to understand what they were saying but aware of their new alertness.

'I think the water's hot enough now,' she said, standing up. 'I'm going to rig it up for my shower. Now, kids, it's bedtime. I know you could go on half the night, but I'm half dead. I'll just expire if I don't get to lie down soon.'

4

PRESENTS FOR AFRA

When Afra woke up, the grey light of early morning was penetrating the little whitewashed room through the thin cotton curtains. She lay still for a moment, feeling snug inside the white cocoon of her mosquito net.

It's my birthday! she thought, a bolt of excitement surging through her, but then she remembered.

Prof, you promised. You *promised*, she thought miserably, and turning over, away from the window, buried her face in her pillow.

A rustling noise came from the door and then a muffled giggle.

'Who is it? Go away,' sniffed Afra, wiping her arm across her wet cheeks.

There was a moment's silence, then Joseph's strong clear voice, and Tom's hoarser one, started singing:

> *Happy birthday to you.*
> *Afra Tovey's a dude.*
> *She's a raver and we love her,*
> *Happy birthday to you.*

The door burst open.

'We couldn't wait. We wanted to give you our present,' said Tom.

Afra sat up and scrambled out from under her net. Tom and Joseph looked so funny standing in the doorway with a messy parcel in their hands that she couldn't help bursting out laughing.

'We made it,' said Tom. 'It took ages.'

Afra took the parcel and unwrapped it.

'What is it?' she said, looking down, puzzled, at the wooden box in her hands.

'Turn it over,' said Joseph. 'Look, it's a nesting box. For birds. There's the hole for them to go in.'

Afra set the box down on the floor and looked at it. It was topped by a pitched roof with proper eaves above the entrance hole and a carving of a bird at the top of the little gable.

'I did most of the box,' said Tom proudly, 'and Joseph did the carving.'

Afra stroked the perfect little bird with her forefinger.

'It's lovely,' she said. 'I love it.'

'You can put it on the verandah at home,' said Joseph.

'No,' said Afra. 'I'm going to hang it right outside my bedroom window. It'll be the first thing I see in the morning when I wake up.'

Voices outside the window made them all look up. Kamande and Julius were talking.

'What are they saying?' said Tom, who couldn't yet understand Swahili.

'I don't know. I think something about elephants,' said Joseph.

Afra put the nesting box down carefully and followed the others through the sitting room and out of the house into the cool morning air. She stood for a moment in the doorway, breathing in the freshness. The sun was just tipping over the horizon and the world looked as if it had been washed in the night. The sparse clumps of grass that sprouted from the bare earth sparkled with dew and the new growth on the acacia trees glowed emerald green. There was a flash of wings above her and the swift darted into its nest above the door, setting off the strange cries of the babies.

They sound like waves running back off a pebbly beach, thought Afra. I wonder how they do it.

Joseph and Tom had run off round the corner of the house. They were walking back now with Kamande.

'There were elephants here in the compound last night,' Joseph said to Afra.

'I still can't believe it. I didn't hear a thing,' Tom said, frowning.

'You don't, with elephants,' said Afra. 'They're huge but they're very quiet. They put their feet down so softly.'

'Look, Tom,' Kamande said. 'Here, in the dust, by the door.'

They all crowded round and looked down to where Kamande was pointing. A vast footprint, as big as a dinner plate, was clearly etched in the dust.

'Did you see them?' asked Joseph. 'How many are there? Did they break down the fence?' He looked worried.

'No, they are so clever. They just pushed open the gate,' Kamande said. 'I only saw one. I heard a noise and I shone my torch out of the window. I thought there was a big grey wall right outside my room. Then it moved and I could see that it was the side of an elephant.'

'That's incredible!' said Tom, his face red with excitement. 'Where do you think it is now? Can we see it?'

'He is probably far from here,' Kamande said. 'He will not stay in the place where he has spent the night.'

'Good morning, everyone,' said a voice behind hem. They turned. Aunt Tidey had come out on to the verandah. Her rotund frame was draped in a kimono dressing gown covered all over with splodgy scarlet poppies.

Kamande gave Joseph and Afra a warning nudge, and Joseph passed it on to Tom.

'Jambo, Mamma,' he said to Aunt Tidey. 'Did you sleep well?'

'I certainly did,' said Aunt Tidey, with a yawn. 'It's so wonderfully quiet here. Mind you, I was so tired it would have taken a herd of elephants to wake me.' She peered at Tom and Afra, who were making strange snorting noises. 'Are you all right? I can't see you properly until I put my lenses in. You didn't catch colds in the night, did you?'

'Oh no, Aunt Tidey,' gasped Afra, pinching herself hard to stop herself laughing. 'We didn't catch anything in the night. I mean, there was nothing around to catch. I mean— Ow!'

She stopped as Tom trod on her foot.

'Well, anyway,' said Aunt Tidey. 'Happy birthday, dear. Now come inside, all of you, and let's get some breakfast. Then we can think about what to take on our picnic.'

The kitchen in the house was small and when breakfast was over and everyone had crowded into it there was very little room.

'Now!' said Aunt Tidey. 'We must make sandwiches. Afra, get the bread, and Tom and Joseph, you'll find ham and cheese in the icebox.'

'I have made the sandwiches, Mamma,' said Kamande. 'Look, they are ready.'

He opened a plastic box and showed Aunt Tidey a neat stack of sandwiches. Aunt Tidey's eyes opened wide.

'Goodness. How very efficient of you,' she said.

'The salad is in this box,' Kamande went on,

'and in the basket there is the fruit, and the special biscuits that Sarah has made.'

'But when did you do all this?' cried Aunt Tidey. 'We've only just finished breakfast.'

Kamande grinned.

'When we go off on a dig with Professor Tovey we must start early in the morning. I always help to make the lunch for all the archaeologists, and then I drive them out of the camp to the site. I am used to getting up with the sun. It is better to go out early in the day. We also should go out now, before it is too hot.'

Aunt Tidey stared at him in admiration.

'Richard was right,' she said. 'You're a much better person to have around on a trip than he is. I don't believe he's ever put a sandwich together in his entire life.' She sensed Afra bridling beside her. 'Oh!' she said brightly. 'There you are. Come with me to my room, dear. I have to give you your present before we go out.'

Afra followed her down the corridor to the little room at the end of the passage. Aunt Tidey had made her bed, tucking the corners in with extreme neatness. A row of bottles and sprays stood on the table under the window, ranked in order of size. Her kimono hung on a coat-hanger behind the door and a book lay perfectly square beside a torch on her bedside table. Aunt Tidey saw Afra looking round and laughed a little defensively.

'Well, it's just the way I am,' she said. 'I do like to be neat. If I didn't keep things under control I'd just get too horribly confused. You wouldn't believe this, honey, but inside I'm just terribly disorganized. Postively chaotic.' She bent down to straighten the slippers that were already precisely placed side by side under the bed. 'Now, let's see. What have we here in my bag?'

She sounds as if she thinks I'm five years old, Afra thought, wrinkling her nose at the strong smell of rose-scented soap emanating from her aunt's open suitcase, but she couldn't help feeling a little excited. She'd never had a present bought in America before. Aunt Tidey usually sent money at Christmas and on birthdays and she and Sarah went together to spend it on clothes.

Aunt Tidey turned round and put a parcel in Afra's hands.

A book, thought Afra.

She tore the paper off.

'I do so hope you like it,' said Aunt Tidey. 'Richard wrote me how much you love nature.'

Afra opened the book and leafed through it, trying to hide her disappointment. It was big and full of brightly coloured cartoon drawings.

Mrs Elephant sure loves her new little baby girl, she read silently. *She nudges her up onto her feet with that oh-so-useful trunk of hers.*

She shut the book again.

'Thanks,' she said.

43

'A good book's a friend after all, isn't it?' said Aunt Tidey, watching her a little nervously.

'Oh yes,' mumbled Afra.

Aunt Tidey turned away.

'Now what do we need for today?' she said, resuming her bossy voice. 'Sunhat, sun cream, something for stings and bites, my camera . . .'

Afra watched her fussing round the room. She couldn't hide the truth from herself any longer. She was very disappointed in Aunt Tidey. She'd imagined someone completely different, someone tall and elegant, like she'd always imagined her mother to be, someone fascinating and deep, who would instantly understand Afra's inner thoughts and feelings, whom Afra could love wholly and perfectly at once, and who would love her wholly and perfectly back.

She'd hoped above all that Aunt Tidey would tell her things about her mother. Had she really been so beautiful? Had she and Prof loved each other desperately? How exactly had they met in the first place? Hadn't it been difficult for them, Prof being a white American and Sablay being an Ethiopian? And why wouldn't Prof ever, ever talk about her?

But she couldn't bring herself to ask this plain, fussy, overdressed woman about such sacred mysteries. There was nothing a person like Aunt Tidey could say that would illuminate the secrets of the past.

'I'll go get my hat,' she said, suddenly wanting to escape from the oppressive little room.

'I saw it on a chair in the sitting room,' said Aunt Tidey, blinking at her, and Afra saw that she too was disappointed.

She knows I didn't like my present, she thought.

Aloud she said, 'Thanks a lot for the book, Aunt Tidey. It's nice,' and she ran out of the room.

5

THE INJURED BABY

Kamande climbed into the driver's seat of the Land Rover and switched the engine on.

'Everybody is here?' he said, looking over his shoulder. 'Where is Tom?'

'Here he comes,' said Afra, looking back at the house. She leaned out of the window. 'Where's your sunhat? And your sun cream? And your stuff for bites and stings?'

She shot a look at Aunt Tidey, who hadn't seemed to hear her. Tom hopped into the Land Rover beside her. Kamande let out the brake and drove off.

'Sorry to keep you waiting,' he said. 'One of the little swifts fell out of the nest.'

'Oh no!' said Afra. 'Stop, Kamande. We have to go back.'

'It's OK,' said Tom. 'I put him back.'

'Was he OK?' asked Afra. 'He hadn't broken his leg or anything, had he?'

'Don't think so,' said Tom. 'He seemed all right. The minute he was back in his nest he opened his beak and started bawling for food, just like all the others.'

'I understand how he feels,' said Joseph. 'I'm always hungry too.'

'You won't be hungry when we've had our picnic,' said Aunt Tidey, nodding. 'We have enough food to feed the US army.'

It was a good half-hour drive up to the picnic place by the rocky outcrop and the track was rough and slow. Fine dust blew in through the open windows, coating everyone's clothes and hair. Aunt Tidey closed her window and turned round as if to ask the three in the back to do the same, but then she thought better of it.

Tom scanned the bushes eagerly on each side, hoping to see some animals. Twice a kind of antelope ran right out in front of them.

'Impala,' said Kamande, stopping the Land Rover and switching off the engine, 'and look, under that bush. A porcupine.'

The porcupine looked round at them, its dignity unruffled, and in the silence they could hear a dry rattling noise as it shook out its quills and stalked away.

Elephants, I want to see an elephant, Tom said to himself, over and over again.

Once he nearly grabbed Kamande's shoulder as he saw something big and grey and round in the distance, but a few moments later he realized it was only a rock and he sat back again, glad he hadn't made a fool of himself.

They arrived at last at the foot of a steep slope

covered in a rough growth of thorny bushes and a few low trees.

'We can walk from here,' Kamande said, stopping the Land Rover and turning off the engine.

Aunt Tidey looked doubtfully up the hill.

'It looks a little rough underfoot,' she said. 'And there doesn't seem to be any shade. Why don't you all go off and explore? It'll be easier if we meet back down here for the picnic. Then we won't have to carry everything up there.'

Afra, Tom and Joseph had hardly waited for her to stop speaking. They had dashed off up the slope towards the rocks.

'I'll wait for you down here,' Aunt Tidey called. 'Be careful, now!'

Tom reached the rocks first.

'I beat you,' he said delightedly, putting one hand out to steady himself against the huge boulder, taller than a house, that crowned the ridge. 'See, Mr African-Olympic-champion-of-the-world, you're not so brilliant after all.'

Joseph shoved him with his shoulder and Tom shoved back. They swayed backwards and forwards for a moment, straining against each other. Tom was the first to stagger backwards. Joseph clapped him on the back.

'Ha ha!' he said. 'I have just demonstrated once and for all the superiority of Africa Man.'

'Der, rubbish.' Tom grinned. 'You ate more breakfast than me, that's all.'

Afra arrived.

'It's so amazing here,' she panted, sinking down with her back against the warm yellow rock and indicating the view with a wave of her hand. 'Look.'

The others sat down beside her and looked out across the vast panorama of hills and valleys that swept away up to the peak of Mount Kenya. Kamande was still coming slowly up the slope towards them, and beyond him, a long way down, they could see the flash of Aunt Tidey's large white hat as she wandered about near the Land Rover, looking down at the ground as though she was searching for something.

'This is the kind of place where outlaws would hide out,' said Tom. 'You'd get a brilliant view of your pursuers on all sides, and you'd be able to take cover in a shoot-out.' He stood up and slipped into a cleft in the rock face, raising his right hand, then bringing it down slowly with two fingers outstretched as if he was pointing a gun.

'Hey! Ugh!' He suddenly ran out, wiping something off his face with the tail of his T-shirt.

'What happened?' said Joseph.

'That bird,' said Tom, pointing an accusing finger at the raven who was hopping clumsily about on the rock above the cleft, 'he's done his business all over me. Look.'

'Oh my, what a mess, Tom. You should have

worn your hat like I told you,' said Afra, copying Aunt Tidey's voice.

'And put on your bird repellent,' said Joseph.

'And covered myself in a poo-proof mosquito net,' said Tom.

They all burst out laughing.

Kamande's head appeared from below as he walked up the last few metres of the slope.

'It is not good to laugh at Mamma,' he said disapprovingly. 'She is a very kind, nice lady.'

'We weren't laughing at her,' said Joseph. 'We were just, well . . .'

'Laughing at her,' said Afra.

'I'm going to explore,' said Tom. 'Are you coming? Let's climb the rocks.'

He went round to the side of the biggest rock and looked for hand and footholds.

'Is there a way up?' said Afra.

'No, it's smooth,' said Tom. 'You'd never get up there.'

He tried to clamber up a few times, then fell back, defeated.

'I can't do it,' he said. 'Nobody could.'

'Hi!' said a voice above them.

Afra and Tom looked up. Joseph was lying on the top of the boulder on his stomach, laughing down at them.

'I have just demonstrated for the *second* time . . .' he began.

'Right,' said Tom. 'I'm going to get you. Watch this.'

He took a few steps backwards and ran at the rock, leaping up at the last moment to grab a high handhold. He hung there helplessly for a moment, then lunged out with his feet till he found a foothold.

'Are you crazy?' Joseph was peering anxiously down at him. 'You will fall! You will take away all your strength!'

With another huge effort, Tom shot up over the top of the rock and, scarlet-faced, dropped down beside Joseph.

Afra was sitting beside Joseph already, coolly gazing out at the spectacular view. Tom gaped at her.

'How did you get up here?' he panted. 'You got wings or something?'

'I went round by the back,' said Afra. 'It's easier on the other side.'

Tom grunted disgustedly.

Kamande had reached the top of the hill now. He smiled up at the three of them.

'You look like three baboons,' he said.

'That's right, I forgot,' said Afra. 'You said there were baboons up here, didn't you? I can't see any.'

'Probably we are too late,' Kamande said. 'They have been here early in the morning. Look, there are droppings everywhere. Baboons like to sleep in places like this, but in the morning they go off to look for food. They come back in the evening.'

'What's that noise?' said Afra, cocking her head to one side. 'I heard something.'

'It was that goshawk, I think,' said Joseph, pointing up to a great bird who floated on sail-like wings overhead. 'Come on, fast boy. Can you see that big tree there, halfway down the hill behind us? I'll race you to it.'

'OK, big head,' said Tom. 'On your marks! Get set! Go!'

They slithered off the rock and began to hare across the rough ground towards the big tree.

Afra had gathered herself for the race too, but the crying sound had come again.

It's an animal, she thought. It sounds like it's lost or hurt or something.

She clambered down off the big rock and began to look around among the heaps of huge scattered boulders. Perhaps I was wrong, she thought, looking up at the goshawk, who was still wheeling around lazily overhead. But the cry came again. It was nearer this time, coming from behind a big round rock. Afra dashed over to it and looked behind it.

A tiny baboon blinked up at her. His black baby hair was so thick that his pink skin shone through it only on his little belly. Terrified, he opened his mouth in a threatening yawn and bared his teeth.

'Hey, little guy,' said Afra softly, sinking down quietly on to her knees. 'I won't hurt you. What happened to you, all alone here? Where's your mom? Where's your family?'

The baby backed away from her against the rock, trembling and grinning with fear. Afra moved silently away from him, but the baby still seemed distraught. He looked from side to side, as if assessing his chances of running away along the side of the rock, seemed to make a decision and took a few wavering steps, then fell backwards as if he had fainted.

Afra heard someone behind her and turned round. It was Kamande.

'Look,' she said, 'a baby baboon. I'm sure he's hurt or sick or something. We've got to help him.'

She leaned forward again towards the baby but Kamande put a restraining hand on her arm.

'Don't touch him,' he said. 'He doesn't know you. You will upset him and frighten him even more.'

'But I can't just leave him here, all on his own, when he's sick,' said Afra, a lump forming in her throat. 'Maybe his family won't come back for him. Maybe they've forgotten about him, or lost him, or they're dead or something, or they just don't care.'

'They'll come back,' said Kamande. 'Baboons

are very devoted to their babies. And even if there has been an accident to his mother, or something like that, what could you do for him?'

'I could feed him,' whispered Afra, keeping her voice low so as not to frighten the baby baboon, whose eyes had flickered open again and who had lurched drunkenly to his feet. 'I could take him home with me and . . . and bring him up, with Kiksy and Stumpy.'

'And what is it like to be a baboon in a human house?' Kamande said, putting his hand on Afra's shoulder and patting it gently. 'When they are babies it is very nice, because they are sweet and funny, like little children, but they get big and strong, and make a mess and take food as they like from everyone. And they get angry and bite, and one day you have to put them in a cage. And it will be like living in a zoo for them. And they will never, never again have their own baboon family and their baboon friends and other baboons to play with. And they won't ever mate and have their own babies in the future and be normal and happy and free.'

'That's horrible,' whispered Afra, whose arms were aching to reach out and pick up the baby and comfort him.

'But it's true,' Kamande said.

They watched as the baby staggered and fell, whimpering, onto a sharp stone.

'I can't bear it. I can't bear just to leave him

like this,' said Afra, trying to control a wobbling chin. 'He's sick! He might die!'

Kamande didn't answer. He was sitting perfectly still, observing the baby baboon.

'He has no broken limbs,' he said at last. 'Look, his arms and legs are OK. And there are no wounds on him, no blood, no scars. He has not been attacked by an animal.'

'But he could have a disease or something,' said Afra.

'Pneumonia and colds are common with baboons.' Kamande smiled as the baby picked himself up, sat down on a smooth flat stone and scratched his head nervously. 'But you can see, he is not coughing. He does not have a running nose.'

The baby, still scratching his head, yelped suddenly and dropped his hand.

'His head hurts,' said Afra. 'Look, he doesn't like to touch it there, at the back.'

'You are right,' nodded Kamande. 'Do you know what I think? I think maybe he has fallen from the top of this high rock, while he was playing, and hit his head.'

'Yes!' said Afra slowly, thinking it out. 'And he knocked himself out, and when he came round the others had gone off for the day. But his mother – she wouldn't have left him, a little guy like this, would she?'

'Maybe she thought he was with someone else.'

'But she'll know now, won't she?' Afra's voice

was hoarse with anxiety. 'She'll realize he's missing now, and she'll be sorry and worried and looking for him.'

'I think so.'

'Because she'll know he's hungry and thirsty and scared. He's so little, he can't survive long without food and water.'

'Baboons don't need much water,' Kamande objected. 'And he'll still be drinking his mother's milk.'

'But he's old enough to eat. Look! He's trying to pick up grass seeds in his little fingers.' She stood up carefully so as not to alarm the baby, who was beginning to relax a little, used to the human presence. 'That's something I can do. I can get him some food. We've got bananas in our picnic. I know he'd love a banana.'

'Afra,' said Kamande. 'Stop! Wait! Do you want this baby to learn to beg from humans? To become a nuisance when people come here to picnic? Teach him to eat your food and he will ask for it from the next people he sees. And they won't like it maybe. People shoot baboons sometimes, you know.'

Afra clenched her fists and glared furiously at him.

'What can I do then? How can I help? You want me to leave him here, don't you? You want me just to watch him being frightened and miserable.'

'Afra.' Kamande shook his head at her. 'You want to help him, but you must do it in the right way. There is one thing you can do for him. Look.' He pointed up to the sky where the goshawk was still circling watchfully. 'You can guard him against his enemies. He's in danger here alone with the hawks in the sky and leopards or hyenas around, who would come here and sniff him out.'

'Right,' said Afra, her angry flush subsiding. 'All right. That's what I'll do. I'll guard this baby. I'll stay here until his mom comes back and if anything or anyone tries to hurt him they'll have to get me first.'

She sat down on a rock nearby and folded her arms.

'Afra! Joseph! Children!' came Aunt Tidey's voice, calling up faintly from the Land Rover below. 'Come down here now, all of you. The picnic's ready.'

6

THE PICNIC

Afra stood up and looked down the hill towards where Aunt Tidey was standing by the Land Rover, waving both arms above her head. Then she turned her back and sat down again.

'I'm not going to her picnic,' she said. 'I'm staying here with the baby.'

Kamande was looking round behind the boulders, signalling to Tom and Joseph.

'You can go,' he said to Afra. 'I will stay here.'

'I'm not going,' said Afra again.

Tom and Joseph came running up.

'Is the picnic ready?' said Tom. 'I'm starving.'

'Sh! You'll scare him,' hissed Afra. 'Look, there's a sick little baby baboon here.'

Tom and Joseph dropped down beside her on to their haunches.

'What's happened to him?' asked Joseph.

'We think he hit his head. He's kind of concussed or something,' said Afra. 'I'm guarding him in case that goshawk tries to get him. Or a hyena gets wind of him.'

'There's a whole troop of baboons over there,' said Tom, pointing to the far side of the hill. 'Why don't you pick him up and take him over to them? I bet they'd look after him.'

'No they wouldn't,' said Afra. 'They'd just run away from me. Anyway, Kamande says I'd terrify him if I tried to pick him up. But maybe if I just stay near him he won't be so afraid. You go on down. I'm staying here.'

'Are you crazy?' said Tom. 'It's your birthday picnic. There's a cake and everything. She'll do her nut.'

'You can go,' Kamande said, frowning at Afra. 'You do not want to upset Mamma. I'll stay here.'

'I told you.' Afra stared at the three of them mutinously. 'I'm not going.'

'We'll take it in turns,' began Tom. Then he saw the look in Afra's eye and shrugged. 'OK. Suit yourself. Come on, Joseph.'

Joseph hesitated.

'It's not right,' he said. 'I can stay and guard it. Tom or Kamande can stay and guard it. You'll make us all unhappy if you don't come.'

Afra felt fury well up inside her, then slowly subside again.

'All right,' she said. 'All *right*. I'll come back up as soon as I've eaten.'

Kamande sat down, relieved, on a rock.

'Go on,' he said. 'Don't keep Mamma waiting.'

Afra took a last look at the little baboon. He

was holding his tail in his hand, hugging himself with the other arm as if for comfort.

'I'll be back, little guy,' she promised him. 'You take care now.'

Reluctantly she set off down the hill in Joseph's wake.

Aunt Tidey had laid a tablecloth out on the ground and plates of sandwiches, salad, biscuits and fruit were set out on it. Tom was already perched on a fallen rock, leaning forward over the spread and piling food onto his plate. The cake tin, still unopened, stood in the centre of the cloth.

'Here you are at last!' said Aunt Tidey. 'I thought you were staying up there for ever. Tom told me about the little baboon. You didn't touch it, honey, did you?'

'Of course I didn't,' said Afra irritably.

'I'm not sure if rabies is a problem with baboons,' Aunt Tidey went on, helping herself to an egg sandwich, but there are all kinds of other infections, and lice and fleas are—'

'I wouldn't care,' said Afra fiercely. 'He's a baby. He's in trouble.'

'Oh sure,' said Aunt Tidey hastily. 'Tom tells me you were doing a great job scaring away a hawk.' She hesitated between a bowl of salad and a plate of sausage rolls and pushed the sausage rolls towards Afra. 'Try one of these,' she said. 'Sarah says they're your favourite.'

Afra looked at her aunt. She's trying to be nice, she thought. But it was unbearable sitting here, politely eating this unwanted picnic, when every bit of her wanted to be with the baby baboon, guarding him, protecting him, keeping him company through the lonely frightening day. And I'm not even hungry, she thought.

She ignored the sausage rolls and picked up a crisp.

'What's it like if you're concussed?' she said.

Aunt Tidey was pouring drinks out into plastic tumblers.

'You feel a little wobbly for a while,' she said. 'And you certainly have a headache. But after a day or two most people are just fine.'

'My friend Scott was concussed once,' interrupted Tom, stuffing a third sausage roll into his mouth. He chewed rapidly for a moment and swallowed. 'He fell off his bike and bashed his head on a kerbstone. Nearly cracked it open. He was sick and everything. Mum said you have to be dead careful with concussion, to rest and not jump around, but if you drop off into a deep sleep you have to keep being woken up in case you go into a coma.'

Afra jumped to her feet.

'I'm going back up there,' she said. 'Thanks for the picnic, Aunt Tidey. I guess I'm just not hungry.'

Tom glanced up at her, aware that he had said

something wrong, but not sure what it was. Aunt Tidey looked at her in consternation.

'But the cake!' she said. 'You haven't even had your cake!'

She leaned forward, her plump forearms quivering, and took the lid off the cake tin with a flourish. In spite of herself, Afra leaned over to look at it. She wasn't used to birthday cakes. She didn't know what it would be like, but at the sight of this stodgy looking square with yellow icing dripping greasily down the sides she felt a sharp pang of disappointment.

'It's a carrot cake,' said Aunt Tidey. 'The frosting's melted a little, but I'm sure it tastes good. It's an old recipe of my mother's, your grandma, Afra. She used to make this cake for me when I was a little girl.' She lifted the cake out and put it down on the tablecloth. 'I thought we'd just put the finishing touches on it here.'

She fished into the bag beside her, pulled out a packet of brightly coloured hundreds and thousands and scattered them on to the cake, then planted a single candle in the middle of it.

'This was the only one I could find,' she said.

Tom, about to describe the incredible Dracula cake Scott's mum had once made, thought better of it. He'd been having such a good time all morning with Joseph that he hadn't noticed much else, but it was impossible now to ignore the electricity that was crackling out of Afra.

Aunt Tidey lit the candle and smiled up at Afra, inviting her to blow it out. Afra stood still. She wanted to pick the dreadful birthday cake up and hurl it as far away as she could. She wanted to shout something rude and run away. But she could see a new alertness in the boys' faces as they looked at her and she didn't want them to think badly of her. Ungraciously, she bent down and blew the candle out.

Aunt Tidey laughed self-consciously.

'Just think,' she said. 'I'm your only aunt and in all these years I've never once seen you blow out your birthday candle.'

Afra looked briefly across at her. There was a hurt expression in Aunt Tidey's eyes. Afra sighed inwardly and took the knife Aunt Tidey held out to her. She cut into the soggy cake. Tom politely held out his plate. Joseph put his hand on the ground to steady himself as he leaned forward with his plate, then grunted with pain.

'What happened?' said Aunt Tidey. 'Did you hurt yourself?'

Joseph was examining his hand.

'It was a sharp stone,' he said. 'I cut myself a bit.'

'Oh,' said Aunt Tidey, 'I'm not surprised.' She began ferreting about in her bag. 'Wait, I have a Band-Aid here.'

'It's all right,' said Joseph. 'It's nothing.'

'The stones are so sharp here,' said Aunt Tidey.

'They're quartz mainly. I was investigating them this morning. Malachite with flecks of fool's gold. Very pretty.' Three blank faces looked at her. 'Geology,' she went on, with her little laugh. 'It's an interest of mine.'

The boys' eyes were wandering over the nearby ground.

'Malachite. That's green, isn't it?' said Tom. 'Isn't it valuable? Hey, maybe we'll find a whole lot of it and get rich. Rich!' He did a little jig in front of Afra, trying to make her smile. She looked away from him, up the hill towards the still figure of Kamande, who was sitting by the big boulder.

Joseph had wandered off, cake plate in hand, to look at the ground. Suddenly he pounced on something.

'A cartridge!' he said. 'Look. People have been shooting here.'

'Let's see.' Tom ran over to him. 'Wow! Who were they, d'you think? I said it'd be a great place for outlaws.' He looked around, scanning the empty landscape that rolled away, an unbroken vista of trees and scrub, shimmering now in the noon heat.

Joseph was still examining the cartridge.

'It's from the army. Kamande told me they practise here sometimes.'

'Target practice you mean?' Tom sounded disappointed.

'Yes, only for practice. They're all blanks.'

Joseph pounced again. 'Wait! Look! This is a new one. Unexploded! I've never found one like this before.'

'They're dangerous, aren't they?' Tom leaned over his shoulder to look.

'Only if you drop it in the fire or hammer it down on something.' Joseph pretended to bring the cartridge down sharply on a rock. 'The percussion hammer would go off and it would explode.'

'Be careful!' exclaimed Aunt Tidey nervously.

Afra darted over to the boys, her plateful of cake abandoned.

'How many more of these things are lying about here?' she said, taking the cartridge out of Joseph's hands.

'None,' said Joseph. 'It's very rare to find them.'

'Get on. There are millions, I expect,' said Tom. 'You know what the army's like.'

A horrible picture came into Afra's mind of the little baboon finding something small and round and shiny, something that would perfectly fit his agile little fingers. She could see him playing with it. Putting it in his mouth maybe. Banging it down on the rock. She took off at once and began sprinting away up the hill.

'Afra! Honey! Don't go!' Aunt Tidey started to call after her. But her voice tailed hopelessly away.

7

SHELTER FROM THE MIDDAY SUN

Kamande was sitting with his back against the boulder. He had pulled his peaked cap down over his eyes, which were closed. He opened them when he heard Afra's feet crunching on the stony ground and pointed with his chin towards the hollow where the baby baboon was.

'It is not so good for him now,' he said. 'There is no shadow for him here and he cannot get away from the sun.'

'Then we must fix some shade for him,' said Afra impatiently.

'I have been thinking about that,' said Kamande, 'but it is not easy. We need a big sheet or a blanket but we do not have one.'

'The tablecloth!' The words were no sooner out of Afra's mouth than she had begun to bound down the hill again.

'Afra!' Kamande called her back. 'Stay here. I will go down. I want to get my hat from the Land Rover anyway.'

Afra leaped back up again, then squatted down near the baby baboon, moving slowly and carefully so as not to alarm him. He was looking sick.

He lay curled up against the rock, his tiny legs folded under him. His eyes were shut.

What if he's gone into a coma? thought Afra, anxiety stabbing through her. She hesitated, tormented by indecision. Perhaps she should try to rouse him, to stop him falling unconscious. But if she woke him out of a healthy, healing sleep, she might do him more harm than good.

She shifted her position and her shoe dislodged a little stone that rattled away down the slope. The baby baboon opened his eyes and looked at her. His little body tensed, but she could see that he wasn't as frightened of her as he had been before.

He's getting used to me, she thought.

A fly landed on the baby's long black nose, tickling him, and he brushed it slowly away with his leathery little hand.

He's weaker, thought Afra.

She scanned the sky. There was no sign of the goshawk, but the two ravens were still arguing noisily on the rock above. The sun was almost overhead now, and very hot. Afra stood up and moved closer to the baboon. If she could lean over just a little without falling, her shadow would cover him. She tried it, manoeuvring herself into the best position. The baby watched her through half-closed eyes and struggled to get to his feet, frightened by the big creature standing over him. Afra sat down quickly again. The baby relaxed a little.

'It's OK,' Afra murmured softly. 'You're going to be OK. Just hang in there till your mom comes back.'

There were footsteps behind her and she turned to see Joseph and Tom racing up the hill with Kamande following them more slowly. Behind them, walking more slowly still, was Aunt Tidey, the blue checked tablecloth over her arm.

'How is he?' Tom called out. 'Have you found any cartridges up here?'

Afra turned on him.

'Sh! Be quiet, can't you? Do you want to scare him to death?'

Tom backed away, offended.

'OK. I only asked.' He leaned over to look at the little baboon. 'He's almost like a baby, isn't he?' he whispered wonderingly.

'He *is* a baby,' said Afra vehemently. She didn't understand why she felt so angry with all of them. She just wanted them to go away and leave her to look after the baby on her own.

To her relief, Tom turned away.

'We're going to look for cartridges,' he said. 'To see if we can find any more unexploded ones.'

Joseph was already walking away, his head down, scanning the earth. Afra braced herself to face Aunt Tidey. She wanted the tablecloth as a shelter for the baby, but she didn't want the fuss that would go with it.

'Now then,' said Aunt Tidey breezily. 'Where's the patient?'

'Please,' said Afra tensely. 'Don't make a noise.'

Aunt Tidey tiptoed towards the hollow, moving surprisingly lightly for such a heavy person. She stood for a moment looking down at the baboon.

'The tablecloth isn't going to work,' she said quietly.

Afra nearly stamped her foot.

'Why not?'

'It'll terrify him. This is a wild animal, not some poor creature out of a zoo. He's never seen cloth before, never mind a vivid blue check. Just think how it would seem to him, this big scary flappy thing over his head. It'll be like his worst nightmare of the ultimate bird of prey.'

'OK.' Afra felt like exploding with frustration. 'So we just leave him here in the sun to fry to death?'

'Of course not, honey.' Aunt Tidey was looking around, seeming to ignore Afra's rising temper. 'I just think we need something a little more natural, that's all. A little less threatening. Like one of those bushes over there, for example. If we can cut some branches and put them nearby, he'd be in the shade but he'd feel OK about it.'

'That's it!' Afra felt as if she'd been pushing against a locked door and it had unexpectedly opened. She looked over to the nearest clump of bushes. Kamande was bending over one. He straightened up, a big leafy branch in his hand.

'Seems like Kamande had the idea already,' murmured Aunt Tidey.

Afra ran down to Kamande and helped him break off a few more branches. They carried them back up to the hollow. Afra bent down so as not to alarm the little baboon, and set the branches up in a pile near him. They created a little pool of dappled shade.

'It's still too sunny,' she whispered to Aunt Tidey. 'If we lay the tablecloth over the branches on the far side from him, do you think it'll still scare him?'

'I guess not,' said Aunt Tidey. 'He won't be able to see it.'

Afra stretched the tablecloth over the branches. The shade under them was deep and inviting now. She moved back, and Kamande and Aunt Tidey moved with her.

The baby baboon had been watching the movements round him, making little 'Geck! Geck!' noises of distress, but as soon as the watchers had withdrawn a little, he dragged himself into the inviting patch of shade, sat down, and began to groom one of his skinny little legs.

'It worked!' whispered Afra delightedly.

Aunt Tidey was still frowning towards the little creature.

'He needs food,' she whispered positively.

'Kamande said not to feed him,' said Afra, 'in case he learns to beg from humans.'

Aunt Tidey raised her eyebrows as if surprised at Afra's slowness.

'You don't need to actually *feed* him with your own hands,' she said. 'He doesn't have to know where the food came from. You must use a little subtlety, my dear. Run down to the Land Rover and bring up one of those delicious bananas. You can leave it near him and encourage him to find it for himself.'

Afra suddenly felt a little better. She took off at once down the slope, covering the distance to the Land Rover with long leaps.

'Bring one back for yourself!' Aunt Tidey called softly after her. 'You haven't eaten eat a thing today.'

Afra found the bananas, took two, and hurried back up the slope. She was grateful for Aunt Tidey's help, but she wanted her to go back down to the Land Rover and leave her alone.

'Thanks,' she said awkwardly. 'I can manage fine now.'

To her relief, Aunt Tidey took the hint.

'I'll go and shut my eyes for a little under the tree down there,' she said. 'Don't stay in the sun too long yourself, now, will you?'

She began to go carefully down the slope, picking her way, with her white sandalled feet, between the stones and thorny bushes. Afra sank down with relief onto the ground. Kamande had gone over to the far side of the hill. She could hear him calling to Tom and Joseph. They seemed to have abandoned their hunt for cartridges and were playing some kind of war game, pretending to shoot at each other from the deep gullies gouged out by the last torrential rains.

I bet they're scaring off the baboon troop, she thought irritably. How can they be so stupid? She felt completely out of sympathy with her friends today. She'd never felt so distant from them before.

She stood up and looked round behind the big boulder. She could see the baboons clearly now, far away to the left. They were moving slowly across the open countryside, stopping constantly to forage among the bushes, or to search the ground for things to eat. They were nowhere near the boys.

Afra went back towards the hollow. She was alone at last. She could concentrate on the baby.

Should I peel the banana or just leave it with the skin on? she thought. He's so little he's probably never eaten one. He might not know what to do with it.

She decided to compromise and pulled the skin a little way down, exposing the fragrant soft centre. Then she pushed the fruit under the branches towards the baby.

He looked round at the rustling sound, tense and alert, but didn't notice the banana. Afra waited for a moment, unwilling to frighten him, then picked up a length of soft vine and poked it after the banana. The baby spotted the vine at once and began to chatter and make his little distress calls. Afra twisted it around so it was touching the banana. The baby backed away from it anxiously. Afra kept the vine still and the baby moved forward cautiously and touched it, pulling his hand back at once as if he was afraid it would bite. His fingers brushed against the banana and he lifted them to his nose and sniffed them.

'Go on. It's good to eat. You'll love it,' Afra urged him on in her head, willing him to pick the banana up, but the baby rolled it away from him with his foot, and sat down in his old position, hunched and quiet, as if the exertion of the last few minutes had exhausted him. Frustrated, hot and thirsty, Afra settled down to wait.

8

BIG SISTER

It had been bright all morning and now, in the middle of the afternoon, it was unpleasantly hot but some puffy white clouds had started to blow across the sky, giving some welcome relief from the direct heat of the sun.

Afra sat on her rock near the little baboon.

'She'll come for you. Your mom'll come for you,' she murmured again and again as if she was reciting a magic spell.

The baby had relaxed a little now that things had quietened down. He sat in his pool of shade, sometimes seeming to sleep, sometimes listlessly grooming his fur, or picking up whatever he could reach – little stones, dead twigs or leaves, sniffing them and dropping them again. Time passed slowly.

The goshawk had gone, soaring away on slow lazy wings towards Mount Kenya. Afra envied it. She would have liked to fly away from the whole lot of them; from Joseph and Tom, who were supposed to be her friends and who she could hear now in the distance, laughing and shouting at each other, ignoring her completely; and from

Kamande, who wasn't supposed to be here at all and who couldn't possibly, ever, take Prof's place. Most of all she wanted to fly away from Aunt Tidey, who didn't understand the first thing about her and was pernickety and irritating and bossy and couldn't even choose a decent birthday present or make a proper cake.

My mother would have known what kind of cake I like, she thought.

She sniffed and wiped her nose with the tail of her T-shirt. At night, when she'd been little and unable to go to sleep, she'd often imagined what it would have been like if her mother had lived. She'd made up stories in her head about the three of them, Prof and Sablay and Afra, walking together, all holding hands with Afra in the middle.

Are you tired, darling? Sablay would say. *Jump up on to Daddy's back. He'll carry you.*

Or they'd be staying in a beautiful house in a wonderful place like America or Ethiopia and Sablay would say, *You don't have to go to bed yet, little Afra. Come and sit by me and I'll read you stories until the moon goes down.*

Her mother's face had always been unclear, flat and stiff, like it was in the photograph Afra had above her bed at home, but the feel of her, the sound of her voice and the touch of her arms had been achingly real. She tried to conjure them up now, imagining the picnic she would have had if

Sablay and Prof had been there instead of Aunt Tidey and Kamande, and fell into a sweet, sleepy daydream. It would have been one long, blissful day of perfection, of marvellous games and wonderful presents and a cake that would . . .

Something moved a little way off to the left of her. She was back in the present at once, alert to danger. She looked round, but whatever it was had disappeared behind a rock. Afra jumped up, ready to do battle with a snake or a jackal or a hyena – with anything that would threaten the baby baboon. But it was only a little rock hyrax that scurried out from behind the rock, its whiskered face looking round at her with startled eyes. It dashed down the hill in a blur of brown fur.

Afra followed it with her eyes. A few gazelle had ventured quite near the Land Rover, their small elegant heads lowered to the ground as they grazed. Under a tree she could make out the large pink-clad shape of Aunt Tidey and the round white dinner plate of her hat as she leaned against a big stone with her head back, her book fallen to the ground beside her. Kamande was nowhere to be seen.

Afra sat back against the rock and her own eyes closed. For a while, she slept.

She woke some time later with a start. Her eyes flew at once to the baby. He was huddling close to the rock and he looked so alone and his baby face looked so old and sad that she felt a new rush of love for him.

'I don't care what Kamande says,' she whispered to him. 'I'm not going to let you die. I'll take you home with me if I have to, and I'll make sure you have a happy life. I'll see to it that you never get locked up in a cage, and that you get to be with other baboons and . . . '

'Who are you talking to?' said a voice behind her.

Afra jumped.

'Joseph!' she said, turning on him furiously. 'What are you creeping up on me like that for?'

Joseph frowned.

'I was being careful,' he said. 'I didn't want to scare the baby. How is he doing?'

'I don't know. He's very quiet. He sleeps some of the time, then he gets kind of restless. Where's the troop?'

'They're still moving away down the valley. We followed them a little way. They've spread out a lot. Are you going to stay here? Why don't you come with us for a bit? It's nice down there. Tom and I found another cartridge. Look.' He pulled two little bronze cylinders out of his pocket and looked down at them proudly, separating them out with his forefinger.

'I'm not leaving him.' Afra looked back at the baboon. 'I'm staying here.'

'I could stay here instead of you. It's so boring for you alone here all day.'

'I'm not bored. I'm not alone anyway.'

'Kamande said the troop will turn back in the evening. They'll come back to the rock to sleep.'

'*Kamande* says!' An angry flush rose in Afra's cheeks. 'He doesn't know everything. He says it would be impossible for me to raise this baby, that I would only make him unhappy, but I've been thinking and I—'

'Are you crazy?' Joseph stared at her. 'Raise a baboon? Like a pet dog? He's a wild animal. He's not a toy.'

'How dare you say that? How *dare* you?' Afra's fists were tight balls of anger. 'I've never, ever thought of an animal like that. Are you saying that Kiksy and Stumpy are toys? Are you? *Are* you?'

'No! OK, calm down!' Joseph stepped backwards and put his hands up in a soothing gesture. 'Afra, you're so wild and angry sometimes you drive me crazy. What's wrong with you? I know you wanted Prof to come, but he couldn't, that's all. Fathers don't care about birthdays. When did my father ever come near me on mine? When did he ever come near me at all?'

'You don't understand,' said Afra, a little sob in her voice.

'No, I don't.' Joseph began to walk away. 'I'm tired of you making us all feel bad and giving us a hard time. This is a great place and Tom and I have found so many nice things down there, and Kamande's showing us how to make throwing sticks, and your auntie's trying to do her best for you, but you don't care about any of us. You're just interested in being miserable.'

'OK. I'm sorry. Just leave me alone, OK?' Afra turned her back on him and kicked at the stone she had been sitting on.

'I will. I will leave you alone,' said Joseph, moving away. 'It will be time to go soon, anyway. Kamande wants to get back before the sun goes down.'

'Time to go?' said Afra passionately. 'I'm not going anywhere while this baby's on his own, and you can tell that to Kamande.'

'You can tell him yourself,' said Joseph and he disappeared again behind the big rock.

'Just leave us alone,' said Afra again to the empty air.

She sat down again. Her hands were gripped tightly together and she was biting her lower lip.

'Toys!' she said out loud. 'How could he say that? *Toys!*'

She was so wrapped up in her angry thoughts that she didn't hear the young female baboon approaching from behind the big rock until she was quite near. Then, seeing a movement out of the corner of her eye, she turned her head and saw her. Her heart leapt, and for a moment the girl and the baboon stared at each other. Then slowly Afra backed away, a little further down the hill, so that she could watch the new baboon without disturbing her.

They are going to come back for him then, she thought.

She ought to be overjoyed, she knew, but she couldn't help feeling disappointed. She'd imagined it all – how she'd feed the baby with a human baby's bottle, and train him to live with humans, and then set about introducing him again to the wild.

She looked round. Where were the other baboons? Surely the whole troop usually moved together? She stood up and walked a little way behind the rock. She could just see the small brown figures of the other baboons a long way away. There were none nearby. The little baboon seemed to have come back on her own.

Afra went cautiously back to her watching point. Her movement startled the young female who grunted at her angrily, flashing her startlingly white eyelids up and down in an attempt to scare her away.

Afra sat down quietly. The young baboon ran up to the baby and pulled him into her lap. She looked tense and anxious and seemed to want to carry him away, but he was too weak to cling to her properly. She was too small to carry him without his cooperation and after a few attempts she gave up trying. She tugged at his arm, as if she wanted him to follow her. The baby took a few faltering steps but fell down again, too weak to go any further.

She looks like she's his big sister, Afra thought.

The young female tried again, grabbing the baby by the leg and then the arm, trying to persuade him to come with her, but the baby moaned and kept trying to crawl back to his shady patch below the branches.

Then the baby's sister seemed to notice something. She reached out and picked up the banana. Delicately, she peeled back the skin and began to eat it. The baby, seeing by her example that it was good to eat, wanted to have some too. He watched his sister closely, and when she dropped a piece on the ground, he reached for it, and put it in his mouth.

They looked so funny, like a human brother and sister sharing a treat, that Afra nearly laughed. She wanted to stay and watch them for ever, to see the baby get stronger again now that he had eaten, to watch them scamper off and play together. She settled herself more comfortably on her rock.

A shadow fell across her. She looked up and saw Kamande.

'I told you,' he said, smiling down at her. 'I told you they would come back for him.'

'It's only one of them,' Afra said. 'And she's only little herself.'

'The others may not come back until you have gone.' Kamande squatted down beside her. 'They will not come too close to you. But you can see now that he is all right. I have come to get you. It is time to go.'

Afra sighed. She wanted to refuse, to make a fuss and stay watching the baboons, but Joseph's words were still stinging. Besides, she had no excuse any more. The baby baboon was no longer alone. His own kind would look after him now.

'In a minute,' she said. 'I'll follow you.'

Kamande stood up and Afra heard his feet crunching back down the hillside towards the Land Rover. She fished in her pocket and pulled out the second banana, then, with a long stick, pushed it towards the two little baboons. They didn't notice it. Carefully, Afra threw a little stone towards it. It rattled on the rock and the two baboons turned towards the noise. The female saw the banana at once and pounced on it. She peeled it and began to eat, and the baby climbed into her lap and retrieved the pieces she dropped.

'I guess you'll be OK, little guy,' said Afra, a lump in her throat. 'Goodbye. Good luck.'

She began to retreat back down the hill towards the Land Rover.

9

A RED-HOT BIRTHDAY CAKE

Tom had had a great day. He'd been afraid it would be boring at first, because Afra, who usually had so many ideas of fun things to do, had been so silent and furious. But he hadn't realized how exciting it was, just being out in the African countryside.

As soon as they'd finished their picnic (he'd particularly liked the sausage rolls, and the cake had been peculiar but edible all the same) he and Joseph had gone up to see the baby baboon. They'd soon left Afra on her own with him, and had gone on down behind the hill to look for more cartridges.

Joseph spotted one almost at once. He bent down to pick it up, then crouched down to examine the ground more closely.

'What have you found?' said Tom. 'A diamond necklace?'

'No. Leopard prints,' said Joseph. 'Look. Here.'

Tom bent down beside him.

'I can't see anything.'

'Yes, look.' Joseph pointed out the faint mark of five pads.

'Yeah, I've got it now. That's brilliant. Do you reckon there are any more?'

Joseph chuckled.

'There must be. I mean the leopard didn't just come down from the sky and put one foot on the ground and fly off again, did he?'

Tom ignored him.

'I bet there are other animal tracks round here. All kinds of things. I bet if we really knew how to do it we could follow them.'

'My grandfather can do that.' Both boys were crawling around on their hands and knees now, examining the ground. 'He was a wonderful hunter.'

'Didn't he teach you? I wish he'd teach me.'

'I don't see him so often. He's in his village. We can't go there very often.'

'Why not?'

Joseph shrugged.

'It's far away, and I'm at school and Mama has to work.'

'Looking after Afra and Prof, you mean.'

'Yes.'

They both sat back on their heels.

'Afra's a pain sometimes,' said Tom.

'Yes. When she's feeling bad, everyone suffers.'

Tom remembered something his father had said.

'That's women for you,' he said.

Joseph was following his own line of thought.

84

'Prof's always working so hard. He has to do it. He's a famous archaeologist. But Afra has my ma, and you and me. And her auntie.'

'I don't think she likes her auntie much,' said Tom. 'I do. Like her, I mean. She's a bit wacky, but she's OK.'

'Why is it always Prof, Prof, Prof with Afra?' Joseph went on, taking no notice of Tom. 'I never see my dad but I don't care.'

'Where is he, then, your dad?'

'I don't know. He went to Zambia years ago. He never came back. He had another wife. He didn't care about us.'

'Didn't you get on with him then?'

Joseph snorted.

'I was scared of him. He used to beat me and Ma. I was glad when he went. I don't remember him so well. I was only a little kid. We're better off without him, Mama and me. Uncle Titus looks after us, anyway.'

'He's brilliant, your Uncle Titus,' said Tom enviously.

'He knows everything about wildlife,' said Joseph proudly. 'He's got a degree in Zoology.'

'Would he know what this is, then?' said Tom, pointing to a cluster of hoof marks on the ground.

Joseph burst out laughing.

'Of course! Even I know these ones. They're from sheep. Come on, let's look for the baboons.

Kamande says they must be near here some-where.'

He began to run up to the top of a little rise from where he could look out. Tom followed him.

'There they are!' said Tom, pointing down into the valley. 'Let's get closer to them.'

They moved off cautiously down the slope, not wanting to scare the baboons into flight. The troop had spread out over a wide area and was peacefully foraging for food.

'They've found something they like there. Look,' said Tom.

The baboons had congregated round a clump of rocks that were covered in long trailing vines. They were picking the fleshy oval fruits off, plunging their fingers into them to break them open and nibbling and licking out the contents with their teeth and tongues.

'Must be nice, spending your life like that,' said Tom. 'Just wandering around eating fruit and stuff. Not going to school or anything.'

Joseph looked at him curiously.

'You don't like school?'

'Not much. Who does?'

'It's better to go to school. So many kids here, they can never go to school. But if you don't get an education . . .'

'OK! No, you're right,' said Tom hastily. He had forgotten how serious Joseph always was about school and he didn't want to risk starting him off on the subject again. To Joseph, school wasn't just a boring necessity but a kind of gleaming express train to the future that didn't have room for everybody and that you jumped onto and clung to for as long as you possibly could.

The baboons had finished with the vines and were moving off. One of them suddenly broke away and began to race across the ground and another, screaming furiously, began to chase the first. They reached the tree and hared up it, then jumped down from it again and ran on, bounding over boulders and running up and down steep rocks, leaping into trees and racing about in the branches.

'I wish I could do that,' said Tom.

'I'll race you back up to the rocks,' said Joseph. 'We had better see if Afra wants to come down here.'

'No, I'm too hot,' said Tom. 'You go.'

Joseph came back a few minutes later. He was scowling.

'Afra's crazy,' he said. 'She says if the baboons don't go back for the baby she'll take it home and raise it herself.'

Tom looked interested.

'That'd be brilliant,' he said.

'You don't know baboons,' said Joseph, kicking a stone that shot off down the hillside. 'They become big and dangerous. They're not toys. I told her that. She was wild. She wanted to kill me.'

'Who wanted to kill you?'

The boys looked round. Kamande was coming towards them.

'Afra does,' said Joseph. 'She's in a very bad mood today.'

Kamande nodded. 'Afra is like the little baboon,' he said. 'She feels wounded herself. Everyone feels like that sometimes.' He ran his fingers across his forehead to wipe off the sweat. 'It is so hot here. Let's go and sit under a tree. In the shade.'

The boys followed him to a big old tree whose bulbous grey roots stretched out like giant fingers across the earth. They all chose a root and sat down.

'This is nice,' said Kamande, leaning against the trunk. 'When I was a boy we used to sit under this kind of tree near my village when we were looking after the sheep and goats.'

'Didn't you get bored, sitting there all day long?' asked Tom.

'No. We used to make things. Throwing sticks and things like that. I'll show you how to do that if you like. And we used to practise wrestling. Anyway we had to watch out all the time in case of dangers. There were lions and leopards and hyenas to take our sheep.'

'You used to guard sheep with lions and leopards roaming about the place? And you only had spears?' said Tom. 'How old were you?'

'Four, five, six. We were small kids.'

'Wow.' Tom looked at Kamande in amazement. 'When I was four,' he said, 'I was flicking paint at Scott off my paintbrush at Lee Grove Nursery School. I'd have died of fright if I'd seen a lion. I still would.'

Kamande smiled at him.

'The worst is not in the daytime,' he said. 'You can make a noise and throw your spear and usually the animal is frightened and he runs away. But at night-time, if you are outside, then you are very frightened. You cannot see, and the animals are hunting.'

Tom shivered in spite of the heat.

'My grandfather told me he was lost in the night once, outside in the bush,' Joseph said. 'He was very afraid. He couldn't find his way home. His father went out and lit a big fire for him so that he could see it. My grandfather saw the fire from far away and in that way he found his way home.'

There was silence while they thought. No one said anything for a while. Tom was thinking about a kid of four facing up to a leopard with nothing but a spear in his hand. There'd been a leopard recently, in the forest near his house in Nairobi. He wondered where it was now.

'You said you'd show us how to make throwing sticks,' he said at last.

'All right,' said Kamande. 'Let's go and look out for some.'

It was a long job, finding a suitable bush and cutting the sticks and shaping them properly, and when they had finished, the sun was already dropping slowly down towards the horizon. The harsh light of midday had gone and the colours had intensified. The earth was a richer pink now, sparkling with crystalline stones, the trees a more succulent green, the sky a deeper blue.

'It's so nice here,' said Joseph, lifting his stick to his shoulder for one last try at a throw. He couldn't seem to get a decent shot with it somehow, not like Kamande, anyway, who could make his skim through the air, as straight and true as an arrow.

'Yes,' said Tom, who had given up the attempt to finish his own stick. 'It's great here. I could stay for ever.'

'But we cannot. We must go back,' said Kamande, getting reluctantly to his feet.

'You'll never get Afra to leave her baboon,' said Tom.

'We will see,' said Kamande.

'Do you want us to try and persuade her?' said Joseph.

Kamande shook his head.

'No. Leave it to me. Go back to Mamma. She

must be wondering where everyone is. I will talk to Afra.'

The boys got up and began to wander slowly up to the crest of the hill and down towards where the Land Rover was parked on the other side.

'I really like Kamande,' said Tom. 'He knows so many things.'

'Yes. He's so nice.' Joseph looked up towards the rocks. He could see Kamande squatting down beside Afra. 'But he'll never make Afra leave that baboon. Once she's made her mind up, she won't move.'

They ran down the last few metres to the Land Rover. Aunt Tidey had woken up. She was standing under the tree where she had been sleeping, yawning and stretching her arms above her head.

'My my,' she said, as the boys came up to her. 'To think I've slept all afternoon. That's what jet lag does for you. Takes years off your life. You boys must be starving. It's hours since you ate anything. Let me see now, where did I put those cookies? And the sodas? I'm sure you'd like some.'

'Yes please, Mamma,' said Tom cheekily.

'Oh now,' said Aunt Tidey, beaming at him. 'Don't you go calling me Mamma too. It's bad enough from Kamande. You can call me Tidey, same as everyone else. Why, here comes Kamande now.' She raised her voice. 'Is Afra still up there with that poor little baboon?' she called up to him. 'She didn't stay there all this time, did she?'

'She is all right,' said Kamande tranquilly, taking the keys of the Land Rover out of his pocket and jumping into the driving seat. 'She is coming.'

Tom and Joseph looked at each other incredulously.

'How did you persuade her?' said Tom.

'I didn't.' Kamande smiled. 'Another little baboon came back to look for the baby. They are together now. They do not need Afra any more. She knows she must leave them.'

'Here she comes,' said Aunt Tidey softly.

Afra came bounding down the hill. She stopped a little way from the Land Rover and said, 'I'm really sorry, Joseph, I was horrible to you. I didn't mean it. And I'm sorry, Aunt Tidey. It was a lovely picnic. It was very kind of you, really it was.'

'Oh honey!' Aunt Tidey's face was shining now with pleasure as much as with heat. 'That's gracious of you to say so when after all my efforts it was the worst cake I ever made in my life. I'm so glad you didn't taste your piece. I tried it after you all had gone and I guess I must have put chilli in it instead of cinnamon by mistake.'

A peculiar expression crossed Kamande's face.

'You did?' he said.

'And you ate your entire piece,' said Aunt Tidey apologetically.

'I thought it was all right,' said Joseph.

'So did I, sort of,' said Tom.

Kamande was beginning to laugh, a deep laugh that welled out of him like water from a spring.

'Red-hot birthday cake!' he said. 'I can tell you now – it was horrible! Horrible!'

'Spicy sponge!' giggled Tom.

'Chilli cheesecake!' guffawed Joseph.

Afra felt something beginning to melt inside her.

'Pepper pie,' she laughed.

Kamande turned the key in the ignition and revved up the engine.

'Get in, all of you,' he said. 'It's time to go.'

The Land Rover began to bump away down the track. Afra turned for one last long look at the baboon rock, and she saw a sight that made her heart stand still. The young female baboon was running away from the rocks alone. The baby was all by himself again.

'Stop the car, Kamande!' she shouted. 'We've got to go back! Oh please, please, stop the car!'

10

A DESPERATE PLAN

Kamande looked quickly over his shoulder, saw the little baboon running away and turned his attention back to the road.

'Afra!' He spoke quickly and quietly in Swahili. 'Listen to me. You are being unreasonable. You know that we have to return to the house now before it is dark. There was an elephant around here yesterday. It may come back tonight. There is the safety of your aunt and your friends and all of us to be considered.'

'But I can't just—' said Afra.

'And anyway,' Kamande went on, 'if you stay near the rocks the baboons may not return. You will be preventing the mother from coming back to the baby.'

'But—' began Afra again.

'No.' Kamande spoke with quiet authority. 'We are returning now. We will come back if you like early tomorrow morning.'

Aunt Tidey had been looking back too, trying to see whatever it was that had upset Afra.

'What is it, dear?' she asked. 'Did you leave something behind?'

'Yes,' said Kamande with finality. 'She has left some of her clothing behind. We will return for it tomorrow morning.'

'And the tablecloth!' said Aunt Tidey. 'I quite forgot about it. I don't suppose there'll be much left of it. There are so many wild creatures around here it's sure to be torn to shreds.'

Afra twisted her hands tightly together in her lap. There was no point in arguing with Kamande. There was no point in trying to make any of the others understand either. For a little while, back there, she'd begun to feel better, but now she felt terribly alone again. The thought of the baby baboon, abandoned even by his sister, filled her mind. She could see his sad little face, his weak questing fingers, his pathetic attempts to hug and comfort himself.

I won't let you die. I won't let you be lonely and abandoned, she kept saying to herself.

A desperate plan was forming in her head. The journey by Land Rover back to the house would take about twenty minutes, but progress was very slow because of the ruts and potholes. It wouldn't take much more than an hour and a half to cover the same distance on foot. If she took the torch she was sure she could follow the track in the dark and once the moon had risen it would be easy to find her way back up the path to the baboon rocks.

Her stomach was already turning over with

fright at the idea of being out alone in the dark night. The boys had mentioned leopard tracks on the far side of the hill. There were likely to be lions around too and if she ran into elephants... Worst of all, though, would be the things she might encounter underfoot. Snakes sheltered during the day from the heat of the sun, but they'd be out at night. There could be puff-adders around, or even spitting cobras.

She shuddered.

Aunt Tidey, turning round at that exact moment, noticed.

'Not cold, honey, are you?' she said.

'No no,' said Afra, trying to summon up a smile. An idea occurred to her. 'I've got a headache though.'

'I'm not surprised.' Aunt Tidey nodded. 'It must've been scorching hot up there by those rocks and you haven't had enough fluids today. Here, take the bottle. Have a good long drink.'

She passed the water bottle into the back seat. Obediently, Afra drained it. She was thirsty, she realized that now. She was hungry too. She made another alteration to her plan, then turned her head to look out of the window. She would have to take careful note of the way, of any especially large trees, or sharp bends in the track, or particularly deep potholes. She would need landmarks to find her way back in the dark.

They arrived back at the house just as the sun

touched the horizon. Julius was standing beside the fire outside, poking sticks under a large pot from which steam was already escaping. He looked up slowly when he saw them coming and lifted his hand in a shaky wave.

'What a wonderful thought,' said Aunt Tidey, climbing stiffly out of the Land Rover. 'Tea and a shower. This place is just as good as a top class hotel. Where are you going, dear?'

'To lie down,' said Afra, putting a hand theatrically up to her head. 'This headache's killing me, Aunt Tidey. I think I'll go to bed straight away.'

'Poor baby.' Aunt Tidey put her arm out as if to give Afra's shoulders a squeeze, but thought better of it. 'I'll creep in in a little while with some supper for you on a tray.'

'No!' said Afra hurriedly. 'Please don't. Maybe I'll take something from the kitchen. I'm not hungry. I feel a little sick actually. I just want to sleep. And my door's so creaky it'll wake me up if you open it.'

Aunt Tidey's soft pink forehead was wrinkled with concern.

'You just go to bed then, honey. Sleep it off. Nature's way is best. And I hope you'll feel better in the morning.'

Unable to stop herself, in spite of Afra's rigid face, she bent over and planted a soft kiss on Afra's cheek. Afra felt a pang of guilt shoot through her, but she stifled it and went quickly to her room. She looked round, thinking clearly and rapidly. She would need food, a torch, and proper shoes and socks. She would need a warm sweater and long trousers as well. The temperature would plunge once the warmth of the sun had gone.

She piled the things onto her bed and opened her door a crack. Aunt Tidey was in the shower already. Afra could hear the water splashing and the squeak of Aunt Tidey's feet on the surface of the bath. Julius was still outside, tending the fire, and Kamande was doing something under the hood of the Land Rover. Joseph and Tom were there though, right outside her room, slumped in the old sofa with the broken springs. Tom looked up.

'You OK?' he said. 'Thought you had a headache.'

'I have,' said Afra. 'I'm just going to get something to eat from the kitchen, then I'm going to bed.'

'Are you going to miss supper?' said Joseph, surprised. 'It's going to be frankfurters and fries. I heard her say so.'

Afra pretended to be sick.

'Don't talk about food. I'll throw up. I just want something small to settle my stomach.'

She went through the sitting room to the kitchen.

'It's still a bit light out there,' she heard Tom say to Joseph. 'Fancy a game of football?'

'It's too late. It will be dark in ten minutes.'

'Yeah, but the ball's white. It'll show up in the dark. Come on. It'll be fun.'

The sofa springs twanged as he stood up.

'OK,' said Joseph. 'Let's give it a try. Where's the ball?'

'In our room. Under my bed.'

Their footsteps receded down the corridor.

The kerosene lamps hadn't yet been lit and Afra could barely see. She felt around among the groceries piled up on the kitchen table, and took a packet of biscuits and a couple of slices of bread. There was some cheese somewhere, she knew, but she'd need a knife to cut it and she wasn't sure where the knives were. Time was running out. The splashing of the shower had stopped. Aunt Tidey must be drying herself.

Her hand closed on a bag of carrots. She picked up a couple, held her T-shirt out in front and put them in it together with the bread and biscuits, and darted back to her room.

The next part, she knew, would be the most difficult. She was quite calm, her mind working clearly and fast, as if it was detached from the rest of her. She felt capable of anything, of solving any problem, overcoming any danger.

Quickly she changed into her warm clothes. She'd be too hot for a while, but she'd feel the cold soon enough. She groped around beside her bed for the small bag Sarah had given her at the last minute, in which she'd put some sweets and a couple of cans of Coke. They were still there and she left them in the bag. She'd be glad of them during the night. There was enough room in the bag for the extra food and her torch as well. She stuffed them all in and picked the bag up. She was ready now.

She tiptoed to the door. The bathroom door, which was in the corridor opposite the kitchen, was opening. Aunt Tidey would be coming out and going to her bedroom, which also opened off the sitting room.

Afra heard her slippers slapping softly on the stone floor, and her heart lurched as she realized that the sound was coming closer, right up to her own door.

She took a flying leap on to her bed, dived under the blankets and lay there, quivering with tension. She heard a tiny tap on the door.

'Afra? Are you asleep?'

Afra lay dead still, hardly daring to breathe. There was silence for a moment, then the slippers padded away.

Afra slipped out of bed again. It was now or never. Her aunt was in her own room now. The boys were playing football round the side of the house and Kamande and Julius must be round there too. At any rate she hadn't heard them come in. She opened her door a crack. The creaking of the hinges sounded as loud as a series of pistol shots but she could hear Aunt Tidey humming in a low musical voice in her bedroom nearby. The humming didn't falter. Obviously she hadn't heard a thing.

Afra crept out into the sitting room and shut her bedroom door behind her as quietly as possible. The expanse of floor across to the far side of the room seemed suddenly endless, but she tiptoed across it, holding her breath. She was out in the corridor now.

Suddenly she froze. Someone was coming in through the front door at the end of the corridor, a lamp in his hand. The light was already beginning to throw huge shadows along the walls. As instinctively as a rabbit bolting into its burrow, Afra darted into the bathroom. She stood behind the door, her heart pounding, listening with every fibre of concentration.

Kamande's heavy footsteps went past the bathroom and turned into the kitchen. She heard a slight grating noise as he put the lamp down on the table, then the sound of a drawer being opened and the rattle of cutlery. She knew where that drawer was – on the far side of the kitchen. Kamande must have his back to her.

She opened the bathroom door and scurried out on soundless feet, down the corridor and through the front door. She was out of the house at last, standing on the verandah, trying to control the violent trembling in her knees.

The sun had set completely now and only a thin band of dark red light remained above the horizon. There was still a faint glow from it, and the dark shapes of trees were just visible against the deepening blue sky, but the light was going fast. She could hear the thwack of the boys' feet on the football round the corner of the house and their laughter as they tried to find the ball in the long grass.

For a moment she wanted more than anything else to throw down her bag and run and join them, but then she heard the whirring, cheeping noise of the baby swifts in their nest overhead, and the air was full of wings as their parents swooped in with food for them in their laden beaks. The little baboon's parents might not have swooped back with food for him. He might still be all alone, up there on those rocks, baring his baby teeth in futile defiance at the enemies that would certainly be stalking him now that night had fallen.

A sob rose in Afra's throat and she ran silently across the grass to the gate and out onto the track beyond.

11

PREY!

Her urgency to escape without being caught carried Afra down the first long section of dusty road to the bottom of a little dip, where the track turned a corner before going up the next steep slope. It wasn't until she'd gone up and over the next rise, and the soft light of the kerosene lamp, shining out of the sitting-room window, had disappeared out of sight, that she felt really free.

She had been running, her feet plopping softly in the thick dust, but she slowed to a walk now. There was still just enough light to see her way. The track wound on ahead of her, a pale ghostly ribbon, fringed with thorn bushes which would tear at her clothes, she knew, if she strayed away to the sides.

The air was still warm and heat radiated up from the dust which had been absorbing it all day, but there was a little chill in the atmosphere now. Later it would be cold.

She was encouraged by how familiar the track seemed. She'd only been down it three times, once yesterday on the way to the house, and twice today, on the way to the picnic and back. She was fairly sure she'd find the turn-off towards the baboon rocks. She had watched out carefully on the way home this afternoon and had noticed a big old tree with several dead branches just where the road divided. She knew she'd recognize it again.

The adrenalin that had helped her escape from the house had stopped pumping now. She was calming down. She wouldn't run again unless she had to. It was a long walk to the rocks and she'd need to conserve her energy. Besides, if she went too fast she might stumble off the track.

'Don't worry, baby,' she murmured. 'I'm coming. Just hang on. I'll be there.'

She felt possessed by a steely will, an absolute determination to get back to the rocks, find the baby baboon and save him from the dangers of the night. She might be his only hope of survival. He might be needing her desperately.

The light had almost gone now. She had to admit that she could see almost nothing. She was feeling her way, her feet seeking out the track, whose surface was much harder than the soft earth on either side. She felt something brush across her face and jumped, shaken with fright.

It's only leaves, she told herself. I'm too close to the edge of the track, that's all.

She felt her way back to the middle of it and carried on for a few metres. Something seemed wrong. The track was less obvious than it had been before. It was narrower and rockier.

She reached into her bag and pulled out the torch. She switched it on. The light was dim and wavering and she realized with a shock that the batteries were almost finished. She'd have to use it very carefully and keep it for emergencies. She shone it round quickly and saw that the track had bent round to the right while she'd gone straight on. A few metres more and she'd have lost it altogether.

She retraced her steps.

Take care, she told herself. I mustn't, mustn't get lost.

She switched the torch off and went on, but a little further she sensed something unusual ahead and briefly flashed it on again. The track divided here. One way went up the hill, the other plunged down a steep slope.

Why didn't I notice that on the way home? she thought. She pondered for a moment. I was looking out of the right side of the car, so I wouldn't have seen the track coming up from below because it would have been on the left. Anyway, I don't remember driving up anything that steep. So the right way must be up the hill.

The logic of her decision pleased her and gave her confidence and she set off up the hill with new vigour. But a few minutes later she stopped again. The track had dwindled almost to nothing.

She was going up too steeply, having to negotiate large boulders and big bushes which had certainly not been in the Land Rover's path that afternoon.

She switched the torch on and looked round again. Her heart sank with a frightening thud into the pit of her stomach. She wasn't on the track at all. Somehow she'd wandered off it into the bush.

She tried to control herself, to think clearly, but she couldn't. She was surrounded by darkness, a thick, heavy blackness that was almost suffocating. An awful panic rose up inside her, a terror of the night and all the dangers that lurked in it. In a moment she would be hysterical. Without being able to stop herself she began to blunder back the way she thought she'd come. But it was soon clear that she'd missed the track altogether.

I'm lost, she thought, the words drumming inside her head. I'm lost!

She was standing still now and, no longer distracted by her own footsteps, became aware of other sounds around her. The air had been humming with the noise of crickets but their trilling had momentarily stopped and all around was silence broken only by the faint rustling of leaves in the wind. Then, from far away, she heard a whooping cry, a rising note like a wild unearthly question, and another and another. They faded down into a low growling that sent an uncontrollable shiver through her.

'Hyenas,' she whispered.

She forced herself to think, to make a decision.

I'll keep going up, she thought. The rocks were at the top of a hill. If I stick to the high ground I'll find the way.

It was difficult to start moving again. She felt as if she was standing on a pinnacle with precipices on each side, down which she might easily fall. Danger seemed all around her. The few centimetres of ground on which she was standing felt like the only safe place in this whole terrifying world.

Then, from over to her right, came the drumming of galloping hooves and the crash of breaking bushes. Afra had no time to think or work out what to do. Instinctively she began to run herself, scrambling up the hill, blundering into thorny bushes and half tripping on the rocks and stones. The drumming noise passed close behind her and she turned and saw, in the faint starlight, the dim flash of white markings as a herd of animals bounded away.

'Gazelle,' she muttered shakily, momentarily relieved. 'Whoever's scared of a few gazelle?'

Then another thought occurred to her. The gazelle had been running in the dark for their lives, risking their necks and their delicate legs in their haste to escape. What were they running from? Was there a leopard or even a lion close by?

Her senses were more alert than she had ever

thought possible. Her ears were strained for the slightest sound, her eyes wide open, trying to stare through the darkness, her nostrils flared to pick up any tell-tale scent.

This is what it's like being an animal, she thought. Being someone's prey.

She waited for a long while. She couldn't hear or see or smell anything now that the sounds of the fleeing gazelle had died away but she didn't dare to move.

A feeling of awful desolation swept over her. She truly was alone now.

No one knows I'm here, she thought miserably.

She felt like crying but made herself stop. She couldn't waste thoughts and feelings on self-pity.

She made herself move on slowly and cautiously up the hill, feeling her way with her feet, her hands outstretched to protect her face from twigs and leaves. She was going far too slowly. She'd never make it to the baboon rocks at this rate.

A tiny shift in the darkness ahead brought her to a sudden halt. Something was moving. Something was breathing close by. She froze, her stomach turning to water. Was something crouching, ready to spring? Was a buffalo there, horns lowered, ready to charge at her and trample her to death? She was so frightened she hardly dared to breathe but then a kind of wild arrogance took the place of fear. She was an animal too, a clever strong young animal. She wouldn't give her enemy the advantage of knowing she was afraid.

'Aarghh!' She shouted, rushing forward.

Something towered over her, four long legs as tall as trees, skittering in alarm, and she smelt a sweet horsy breath from nostrils metres above her. Then the giraffe took off along the side of the hill at a rocking canter.

That's all it was, Afra told herself sternly. A harmless old giraffe. That's all it was.

She felt defeated nevertheless. This whole expedition was hopeless. She'd never find her way back to the baboon baby, or even back to the safety of the house.

Then she remembered the torch. What was the point in trying to save batteries for an emergency? This was an emergency, wasn't it? Being lost at night in the bush surrounded by predators was enough of an emergency for anybody. She felt in her pocket and then, with increasing urgency, in her bag. The torch wasn't there. She tried the bag again, feeling into every corner. It was no use. The torch must have fallen out during her mad dash away from the gazelles.

That's it then, thought Afra, sitting down suddenly on the ground. I'm in total, total trouble here.

She buried her head in her arms and at once the tears, which she'd kept back before, started flowing.

'And it's my birthday. My birthday!' she said aloud.

Her words echoed around in the silent night, and somewhere nearby a bird let out an alarmed cry. It jerked Afra out of her tears and brought her fear thumping back with sickening force.

If that was a lion or a leopard chasing those gazelles down there, she thought, I just gave myself away. It'll know where I am now.

Her senses were keenly alert again. She looked round, trying to force her eyes by sheer will-power to penetrate the thick darkness, and noticed something new. A glow had appeared on the horizon, a round aura of light. She thought for a second that an aircraft was approaching, or even that there was a fire on the horizon. Then she realized that the moon was rising.

It came up fast, slipping out from behind the far hills like a pale-bronze balloon floating serenely upwards. The colour changed, turning slowly to silver then to white, and then there was light, a cold unreal light, flooding the landscape and casting shadows of inky blackness.

Afra stood up. She could see. The relief was wonderful. Her fear had receded again, the prickling of her scalp had stopped and the tight band round her chest had loosened. Her knees, which had been weak and trembling, felt strong enough to carry her again.

She scanned the horizon. She had been right to

keep going uphill. From where she was she could see the baboon rocks quite clearly, gleaming eerily in the pale light, and they were not too far away. The Land Rover must have gone a long way round to the picnic spot but it wouldn't take her more than half an hour to walk across country.

While she'd felt so lonely and afraid herself, thoughts of the baby baboon had flown out of her head, but they came back now and she began to walk purposefully, breaking into a run whenever the ground ahead seemed clear enough.

12

AN EMPTY BED

'This is crazy,' Tom said, dribbling the football across the rough ground at the side of the house. 'Do you realize that we're playing in pitch-darkness?'

'Yes I know. It's fun, isn't it?' said Joseph, tackling him expertly for the ball. 'Anyway it's not so dark. There's some light from the lamp in the window, and a bit from the fire too.'

He pulled his foot back for a kick and sent the ball flying, then watched with horror as it made straight for the fire, where Julius and Kamande were sitting together.

'You idiot,' said Tom.

Joseph held his breath. The ball seemed certain to land on the flaming logs but Kamande put up one hand and neatly caught it.

'Come here,' he called out.

The two boys approached him nervously.

'I didn't mean—' began Joseph.

'Don't worry.' Kamande put the ball down beside him. 'Listen, boys, Julius is sick.'

Tom and Joseph looked through the firelight to where Julius sat on the far side. He was wrapped in a thick black and red checked blanket but they could see that he was shivering violently.

'He was in a fever all afternoon,' Kamande went on, 'and then he got up to make the fire and heat the water for us. Now he is very bad.'

'What's the matter with him?' asked Tom.

'Malaria, I think.'

Joseph squatted down beside Kamande.

'Is it serious?' he said softly.

Kamande nodded.

'It can be. He needs medicine. I must take him now to the hospital.'

'Now?' Joseph looked worried. 'You can't drive so far in the dark.'

'I must. Look at him. Listen, Joseph, and you too, Tom. I do not like to leave you here alone with Mamma and Afra, but this is an emergency. You are responsible. Look after them both, OK? Now stay here with Julius while I go and tell Mamma.'

He strode off into the house. He was back a few minutes later with Aunt Tidey at his heels.

'Are you quite sure about this, Kamande?' she was saying. 'I mean is there really nothing we can do to make him comfortable here, at least until it gets light in the morning? I just hate to think of you driving out at night. Why, anything might happen to you.'

'Look at him, Mamma,' said Joseph. 'He must have medicine.'

Aunt Tidey bent over Julius and put a hand on the old man's forehead. She took it off at once and straightened up.

'I'll get you some extra blankets and a pillow to make him comfortable in the car. And water. He must try to drink plenty of water.'

She ran back into the house. Kamande picked the old man up as easily as if he had been a child and carried him over to the Land Rover. Aunt Tidey came out a moment later and tucked the pillow and blankets round him.

'You'll be all right,' she said doubtfully.

'Yes, don't worry, Mamma. You will be all right also. I will return as soon as I can. I will leave Julius at the hospital and return before tomorrow morning.'

'Don't worry about us. See to it that he's OK first.'

Kamande let in the clutch and began to drive off.

'Well now,' said Aunt Tidey, trying to sound bright and reassuring, 'and we haven't even had our supper yet. Come on, boys. I was just putting the frankfurters out on the table.'

She turned back to the house but at the front door stopped and looked down.

'Why Tom, look at this,' she said. 'That little bird has fallen out of his nest again.'

'I'll put him back,' said Tom. 'I know how to now.'

'No, there's no point,' said Aunt Tidey. 'The other chicks will only push him out again. Pick him up and bring him into the kitchen. I guess we'll have to make a nest for him in there.'

Tom picked up the featherless little bird as gently as he could. It lay flopped out on his palm and he could see the pulse of its heartbeat inside its tiny chest.

'I don't think he'll make it,' he said, following Aunt Tidey into the kitchen.

'Nonsense. He's just a little weak from hunger, that's all.' She bustled around picking things up and putting them down as if she was looking for something. Finally she picked up an egg box. 'Take the eggs out of this, Tom. The lid will do fine for a nest. Joseph, cut off the end of a frankfurter and chop it into little pieces. Real tiny ones. OK, now let's give our young friend his dinner.'

She picked up a fragment of sausage and nudged the little swift's beak with it. Weakly it opened its mouth and she dropped the sausage in. The chick seemed to revive at once and its beak gaped alarmingly, while from its throat came a rasping demand for more. The boys laughed and Joseph dropped another morsel in.

'Don't overdo it,' said Aunt Tidey. 'You don't want to kill him with kindness. Bring him to the table. No reason why Jonathan can't have supper with us.'

'Jonathan?' said Tom.

'Jonathan Swift,' smiled Aunt Tidey. 'You've never heard of Jonathan Swift? A great writer. He wrote *Gulliver's Travels*.'

Aunt Tidey, anxious now that Kamande and Joseph had gone, was a little preoccupied during supper, starting from time to time at unexpected noises, but Tom and Joseph were too busy to notice. They were both hungry after a long day out in the open and ate voraciously, demolishing the huge mound of frankfurters and mashed potatoes that Aunt Tidey had piled onto the table. The chick was even hungrier than the boys, and they took it in turns to drop bits of sausage into its mouth. At last it stopped its plaintive cheeping and, completely bloated, settled down to sleep.

'We can't go on keeping it in an egg box,' said Tom, as he and Joseph carried a stack of dirty plates across to the sink. 'What'll we put him in?'

'Afra's birthday present!' said Joseph. 'The nesting box!'

'Of course. Why didn't we think of it before? Where is it?'

'In Afra's room. On the table. It was there this morning, anyway.'

'I'll creep in and get it,' said Tom. 'She'll be dead asleep by now.'

He crossed the sitting room to Afra's bedroom door with Joseph close behind him. Carefully, Tom opened the door, wincing at every creak, and looked inside. The kerosene lamp from the sitting room cast strange shadows across the little bedroom but even so it was obvious at once that the bed was empty and had not been slept in.

'She's not here!' gasped Tom. 'She's gone!'

Joseph pushed past him.

'What? What's happened?'

They looked round the empty room, then turned to look at each other.

'Where on earth is she?' said Tom.

'I think maybe she's gone back to find the baby baboon,' said Joseph. 'You know Afra. She gets an idea in her head and you can't get it out.'

'She'd be crazy! It's totally dark out there! And there are leopards and everything.'

'Joseph! Tom!' Aunt Tidey called from the kitchen. 'Come and eat your fruit salad. It's all ready now.'

'What are we going to do?' whispered Tom frantically. 'Kamande's gone off with the Land Rover.'

'Don't tell her,' said Joseph. 'Not yet, anyway. We must think.'

He grabbed the nesting box off the table and they both went out of the room, shutting the door carefully behind him.

'Oh good. You've found it,' Aunt Tidey said. 'Where was it?'

'Um . . . on the . . . on the table,' said Tom vaguely, putting the box down. 'I'll just go outside and get a bit of stuff to make him a nest. Are you coming, Joseph?'

'Hey, wait a minute!' Aunt Tidey pointed to the boys' empty chairs. 'Sit down. You haven't eaten your dessert.'

Tom and Joseph sat down at the table and hastily ate their way through their portions of fruit salad.

'More?' said Aunt Tidey, her serving spoon hovering confidently over the fruit salad bowl.

'No thanks,' they said simultaneously, pushing their chairs back and jumping up.

Aunt Tidey looked disappointed.

'I thought you boys would just gobble it down. I guess I made too much.'

'We're full of frankfurters,' Joseph said. 'It's very nice. We'll eat it in the morning.'

Aunt Tidey nodded.

'You certainly ate enough frankfurters. All right. Supper's over. Time to clear away.'

'Oh, can't we do it in the morning?' Tom pleaded. 'We're both really, really tired. We'll just go and . . . and look at the stars for a few minutes and then we want to go to bed, don't we, Joseph?'

'What? Oh yes,' nodded Joseph.

Aunt Tidey laughed.

'OK, off you go. I must confess I'm looking foward to bed myself. I'll use the bathroom first. Goodnight, boys.'

She swept the dessert dishes off the table and

put them in the sink, then went into the bathroom and locked the door.

'We must go and look for Afra,' Joseph whispered urgently. 'We're responsible for her. We can't just let her be alone out there.'

Tom shivered. The little house, with its sturdy stone walls and solid front door, suddenly seemed like a safe haven, a bastion of security against the predators that were out there somewhere, on the prowl.

'But it's miles to the rocks,' he said. 'Anyway, we'll get lost.'

'It's not so far.' Joseph was pulling him out of the room. 'We can't talk about it here. *She* might hear us.'

Tom followed him out onto the verandah, and stood beside him, looking into the darkness, feeling his heart sink down into his stomach.

'We'll never find her out there,' he said. 'Never.' Joseph said nothing. 'We'll all three get lost, or eaten or something. It'll just make things worse.'

'You're right,' said Joseph at last. 'We won't find her now.'

'I don't see how she can possibly find her way back to the rocks anyway.' Tom was shaking his head. 'She really is crazy. She must be lost out there herself. And she'll never be able to see the way back here. There isn't even a light we can switch on outside.'

Joseph grabbed his arm.

'You've given me an idea. Do you remember, I told you about how my grandfather's father lit a fire to help my grandfather find his way home? We can light a fire for Afra! She'll see it and if she's lost, it will help her to come back here.'

Tom's heart lifted again. Lighting a fire would be all right. Anything would be better than stumbling about in the dark and getting lost and being eaten alive.

'We must go up to the top of the little ridge behind the house,' said Joseph. 'It would be a good place. It's not far.'

'Right.' Tom's mind was darting forward to think out the details. 'We'll need matches and a torch. What about firewood?'

'There are some dead branches lying around. We'll collect a big pile.'

'It won't be easy in the dark.'

'When the fire's going it will be OK. And we'll need our sweaters. It will be cold soon.'

'Cold?' Tom stepped out from the verandah. The stone walls of the house had retained the heat of the day and it was still very warm indoors. Away from the house, though, he could feel the new chill in the air.

'Come on, then,' he said. 'What are we waiting for? Let's go.'

13

HYENAS HUNTING

It took Afra longer than she'd expected to reach the rocks. The ground was rough, and although the moon was bright she still had to watch carefully where she put her feet. Several times, when she'd had to go downhill, she'd lost sight of the rocks altogether and the awful fear that she was lost again brought her out into a sweat, but each time, as soon as she'd gone uphill, she'd been able to see her way.

A couple of times she nearly ran into a herd of grazing zebra, whose stripes made them almost impossible to see in the moonlight. They scattered nervously at her approach, scaring her as they clattered away on their tough little hooves.

The thing that frightened her most now was the possibility of stepping on a snake. She knew they liked to come out of their holes at night and lie on the warm rocks. The thought that she might tread on one made her skin creep and she gave a wide berth to any long branch lying on the ground which might turn out not to be a branch at all.

She arrived at last at the picnic spot and looked up at the rocks. She could see, even from here, that the baboons had come back. They were sitting together on the very tops of the rocks in closely huddled groups.

Afra felt the same mixture of relief and disappointment that she'd felt when the female baboon had come back to the baby that afternoon. She was pleased, of course she was, that the baboons had returned and that the baby was now no doubt back with his mother. But she'd wanted so much to hold him and make him her own, to feel his fingers clasp her hand and know that he'd need her always.

I've got to make sure, she thought. Maybe they came back but still abandoned him. Perhaps he's still up there on his own.

She was scared at the thought of going too near the rocks. Adult baboons were big creatures. They had long teeth and wouldn't be afraid to use them if they thought they were being attacked. She would have to approach them slowly and cautiously, to look unthreatening and friendly.

She set off up the hill, trying to avoid treading on twigs that would snap or loose stones that would rattle away down the hill and startle the baboons. She kept looking up anxiously at their dim silhouettes. They sat huddled together, putting their backs to the cold wind which had now sprung up and was blowing on them from behind.

At least the wind's coming from them to me, thought Afra. They won't pick up my scent.

One of the baboons noticed her when she was nearly at the base of the rocks. He jumped up and began to run about on top of the biggest boulder, his little body black against the night sky. His barking and cries of alarm woke the others. Afra could see their heads turn as they looked around nervously. She stopped walking, then looked back the way she'd come so that they could see her clearly and realize that she was showing no fear and no interest in them. She waited for a while. The baboons were quietening down again. She tried moving sideways. A ripple of alarm ran through the crowd, and there were one or two short barks but no general panic. She waited again then moved again, not trying to hide herself or be too quiet. This time there was no reaction from the baboons.

They've realized I'm not a threat, she thought.

Slowly she went up the rest of the rise until she was standing at the foot of the rocks. She knew the baboons' eyes were on her and that they were poised, ready to flee or attack if she made a threatening move. Carefully, she walked round to the hollow where she'd left the baby that afternoon.

He wasn't there.

His mother took him then, she thought. Either that or . . .

She didn't want to think of the alternative, of

a hyena creeping up on his horrible stiff legs and snatching the baby up in his iron jaws, or a leopard stalking him on his furry belly, pouncing in a flurry of teeth and claws. If only she could be sure. If only she could make out his little shape in the dark mass of fur above her.

They'll come down off the rocks in the morning, she thought. I'll see him then. I have to make sure. I have to know.

Now that she'd arrived safely at the rocks she didn't know what to do next. The moon was high up now, a brilliant white ball in the sky, too bright to look at, but it wouldn't be there all night. It would set sooner or later and then it would be pitch-dark again.

She looked back over the countryside. She'd never find her way home in the dark. The house was down in a dip and there was nothing nearby that would give her a landmark to aim for. And if she got lost again, and the moon had set and it was quite, quite dark . . . She shuddered. She wouldn't be able to bear it. She'd panic completely and lose control and blunder about and attract every big cat or restless buffalo from miles around.

I'll have to stay here then, she thought.

She sat down on the rock where she'd spent the afternoon, near the hollow where the baby had been. It felt OK here. The baboons might turn hostile if they thought she was about to threaten them but at the moment they felt like company. She could see in the moonlight how close they sat, touching and holding each other, bearing each other company through the long dangerous night.

They're like a big family, she thought, with fathers and mothers and brothers and sisters and uncles and aunts.

At once she thought of Prof.

How could he? How *could* he? she whispered. He knew how much I wanted him to come.

A cry from a young baboon caught her attention and she looked up. One of the huddles was shifting about sleepily, the mass of baboons regrouping itself, drawing even closer together.

They love each other, thought Afra.

She started to cry silently, feeling the tears running down her cheeks. Her nose was running too and she groped in her pocket for a tissue. She had to twist around to get at it and in doing so she looked up.

Far away, on a small ridge that rose a little way above the plain, she could see something flickering.

Someone's lit a fire, she thought, surprised. I didn't know there were people here. They're nomads, maybe. Shepherds or something.

It was comforting to see a fire, even though it was so far away. It made her feel a little less lonely.

The sudden screech of a night bird close by made her jump out of her skin. It was followed almost at once by the whoop of a hyena. The sound was much nearer now than it had been before.

The baboons had heard the hyena too. They shuffled closer together and whimpered.

Afra looked from side to side. If a hyena came up here, there'd be nowhere she could hide.

I should have brought some matches. I could have made a fire myself, she thought. That would have kept them away.

The hyena's unearthly cry came again, followed closely by a second. Afra could see them in her mind's eye, their heads lowered to the ground as they trotted along, sniffing expertly at the trail they were following, their round eyes staring out into the darkness, their jaws dripping hungrily.

Perhaps they're following me, she thought, her heart beginning to thud uncomfortably fast. I must climb a tree or something.

She remembered looking down that afternoon and seeing Aunt Tidey's round form asleep under a big tree with spreading branches which stood above the picnic spot. She'd get down to it now and try to climb it. Leopards could climb trees but hyenas couldn't. She'd be a bit safer up a tree. She went back down the hill to the picnic spot. The tree was big and its trunk was broad and very smooth. The moonlight, bright as it was, was too weak to penetrate its leaves and the shade under it was very dense. Afra felt around for a low branch or boss on the trunk that she could use as a handhold. There didn't seem to be any.

The hyena whooped again. It was much closer now, and definitely coming this way. Fear made Afra strong. She took a few steps back then ran at the tree, caught hold of a stout branch above her head and hauled herself up. She managed to get one leg across the branch and sat astride it, panting, then worked her way back until she was resting against the trunk.

She shut her eyes for a moment while she got her breath back but then she sensed something move beneath her and looked down. The hyena was passing directly beneath the tree, intently following a trail. She could see the rough fur on his ridged back and hear his rasping breath. He caught her scent on the ground and it distracted him for a moment. He circled round under the tree, trying to decipher the smells, snuffling around the roots while Afra held her breath a couple of metres above his head, her eyes round with horror. Then he gave up and trotted purposefully on, back on the tracks of whatever it was he had been pursuing.

Afra let out her breath in a long sigh of relief. Trembling, she wriggled into a more comfortable position against the trunk. She'd have to be careful not to fall asleep and topple off the branch, but at least she'd be relatively safe up here.

Suddenly she was hungry. She pulled the bag off her back, reached inside it and took out the packet of biscuits. The crackling of the paper sounded dangerously loud in the still night air. She started to eat and took a swig out of her water bottle. She'd survive up here all right, until the sun came up and the new day began.

14

HEADLIGHTS IN THE DARK

Joseph and Tom had managed to get up to the top of the ridge without too much trouble. The moon was rising when they left the house and as it grew brighter they could see their way more and more clearly.

'This'll be a good place for a fire,' panted Tom, who had run up the last steep rise. 'Look, there's a dead tree over there and loads of firewood.'

Joseph scuffed the dry twigs and leaves from around some bushes into a pile and carried them out onto a bare patch of ground. They worked hard for a while, collecting wood. Tom took care not to lose sight of Joseph. It was scary, being out here in the African bush at night, with goodness knows how many wild animals so nearby. There was something weird, too, about the moonlight. The shapes of the trees were ghostly and the wind, which had risen now, was moaning through the acacia bushes, making an eerie whistling sound.

Suddenly, something pale flitted up the ridge towards them. It came silently, a horrible, white, fluttering thing. Tom grunted with fright and backed away, stumbling over the rough ground behind him. Joseph had seen it too. Instinctively, the boys rushed towards each other as if for protection. The thing disappeared.

'What was it?' whispered Tom.

Joseph seemed too scared to answer.

A sudden screech from a tree nearby startled them both so much they dropped the logs they were carrying.

'It's a ghost!' Tom's voice was hoarse with fright.

Joseph laughed shakily.

'No, it's an owl. Look, up there on the top branch.'

Tom peered up at the tree. It was a bird all right. He could see it clearly now. It was shifting clumsily from one leg to another, settling its huge wings.

'My grandfather saw a spirit once, a real one, near his village,' whispered Joseph. 'It was a man who had been murdered by his own brother. Grandfather said it was all red with—'

'I don't want to hear about it.' Tom shuddered. 'Come on, let's get the fire lit.'

The pile of wood and kindling was quite big now and the fire took hold at once on the dry tinder. The boys sat down beside it and watched the young flames spurting up, strong and bright.

It was a comforting sight. The fire seemed like a brave companion, a protector, a strong, trusty friend. The boys still felt edgy, looking over their shoulders from time to time down the moonlit slope behind them, but they were no longer really afraid.

'I don't suppose Afra's made a fire,' said Tom. 'We'd see it, wouldn't we?'

'Yes,' answered Joseph. 'Anyway, she doesn't have any matches.'

Tom swallowed.

'Do you think she'll be all right? I mean, there are all kinds of wild animals around here, aren't there?'

'I don't know.' Joseph stirred the fire with his foot. 'She's clever, Afra. She knows animals. But it's still so dangerous for her. We have a fire and we are two. She has no fire and she's only one.'

He shivered. They were both silent for a while.

'What if *she* sees the fire? You know, Aunt Tidey,' said Tom.

'She won't. Her room's on the other side of the house.'

Tom poked another stick into the fire and protected his eyes with his hand as sparks shot up into the air.

'She might. She'll go crazy if she finds all three of us have gone. Maybe we should have told her.'

Joseph backed away from the fire which was scorching his face.

'If Afra doesn't come before morning, she'll find out everything then. What can she do now? If we had told her, she wouldn't have let us come out here like this. Maybe she would have gone out to find Afra alone.'

Tom's forehead was wrinkled with thought.

'I still don't see what's got into Afra. She's been awful all day and now she's gone completely over the top. I know she wanted Prof to come and everything, and she was disappointed when he didn't, and I know she's crazy about animals, and really minded about the baby baboon, but why's she in such a state about it all? I don't get it.'

'She always gets upset about Prof,' said Joseph, putting a bigger log on the fire. 'He's not at home much, and when he is he just works in his study all the time.'

'He's not much of a dad, then?'

'I don't know.' Joseph shrugged. 'I never had a proper one.' He paused for a moment. 'Afra's ma died when she was born. Prof couldn't get over it, Mama says.'

Tom thought about this.

'Maybe he blames Afra or something.'

'Maybe.'

'He's nice, though, isn't he? I mean, he's not mean to her or anything?'

Joseph grimaced.

'No. Prof's great. He's a really, really nice man. He has been much better for me than my own father. It's only that he is . . . kind of unhappy very often.'

They sat in silence for a while. Tom looked out over the cold white landscape.

'You've got to admire her. Afra, I mean,' he

said. 'It was mad going out like that in the night, before the moon came up when it was totally pitch-dark and everything, but it was amazingly brave. She's got more guts than me.' Something caught his eye and he peered out towards the horizon. 'Look, Joseph. See those white things over there? Aren't they the rocks where we were this afternoon? Where we had the picnic?'

Joseph didn't answer. His head was tilted to one side and he was frowning intently.

'Listen,' he said at last. 'Can you hear something?'

'No, what—' began Tom. Then he heard it too. 'Yes! It's a car engine, and look, over there, lights!'

'Kamande must be coming back already,' said Joseph. 'Quick, let's put the fire out and get down to the road. If we can stop him before he gets to the house, we can get him to take us up to the picnic place to look for Afra without telling Aunt Tidey.'

'Good idea.' Tom was already scooping up handfuls of earth to drop on the fire. 'It's a good thing that big log hasn't really started to burn. We'd never put that out in a hurry.'

A few minutes later no trace of the fire remained and the boys were leaping back down the hill. The noise of the car's engine came and went as gusts of wind picked the sound up and carried it away. They reached the track and began to race along it. The sound of the car was coming closer and they could see the lights now too, rising and falling wildly as the car bounced and swerved down the deeply rutted track.

They turned a corner, saw the twin headlights straight ahead, coming towards them quite fast, and jumped up and down, waving their arms to stop it. Then Joseph hesitated.

'Wait!' he called out to Tom. 'That's not a Land Rover. It's a jeep or something.'

He was too late. The driver had caught the two leaping, gesticulating figures in his headlights and had braked sharply, skidding over the last few metres of dust. He wound down his window and leaned out.

'Joseph! Tom! What the hell are you doing out here in the middle of the night?'

It was Prof.

The boys stared at him, astonished.

'Prof! You came after all!' said Joseph softly.

'What's all this about?' said Prof. 'What's going on?'

'We're looking for Afra,' said Tom. 'She's—'

'What?' Even in the dark the boys could see that Prof's brows had snapped alarmingly together above his nose. 'You mean Afra's out here too? Kamande and Tidey have let you kids come out on some stupid game in the dark? Are you all crazy?'

'Kamande's not here.' Tom latched on to the easiest thing to explain. 'Julius has got malaria. Kamande's taken him to hospital.'

'Where's Tidey? Where's Afra?' Prof leaned out of the window of the jeep and looked up at the track as if he expected Afra to step out from behind a tree.

'We don't know,' said Joseph shortly. 'We think she's gone back to the place where we were this afternoon.'

'Where? What place? What do you mean?' Prof's voice was steely.

'There are rocks on the hill,' said Tom. He was torn between alarm at Prof's anger and relief that someone older was taking charge. 'There are baboons there. Afra found a wounded baby.'

'But those rocks are miles away!' Prof glared at Joseph. 'Joseph, how could you take part in all this? You know the dangers. I thought I could trust you.'

Joseph had been looking down at the ground, cowed by Prof's anger, but now he lifted his head and looked Prof in the eye.

'Afra was very very unhappy when you did not come with us,' he said. 'She didn't want to do anything with us. When she found the baby baboon she wanted to look after it, and she wouldn't leave it. Kamande and Aunt Tidey made us come back when it began to get dark but Afra was worried about the baboon. She must have slipped out of the house without telling anyone. We don't know where she is. She was in a very bad state, very angry and miserable.'

'We didn't know she'd gone out,' Tom said. 'We

135

thought she was in bed. We just went into her room and found she'd gone so we came out to light a fire. We thought if she was lost and she saw it, she might to be able to find her way home.'

'And where's Tidey in all this?'

'In bed, I suppose,' said Tom. 'We didn't tell her we were going out.'

Prof jerked his head back.

'Get in, both of you,' he said.

The boys had hardly managed to scramble into the back of the jeep when he took off again, driving so furiously that the jolts threw the boys from one side of the car to the other.

'How long has she been gone?' Prof called over his shoulder, shouting over the noise of the engine.

'We don't know. We didn't go to her room till after supper. Eight o'clock maybe.'

'And it's after midnight now,' Prof said more quietly, as if to himself. 'Four hours.'

The jeep screamed to a halt outside the house. The door was flung open and Aunt Tidey, her voluminous robe flapping about behind her, flew across the grass.

'Kamande! You're home! Thank God! Oh, it's Richard!'

She stepped back as her furious brother leaped out of the jeep and strode up to her.

'Tidey, for heaven's sake, what's going on here? Where's Afra?'

Aunt Tidey wrung her hands.

'Oh Richard, I have no idea! I thought she was in bed, asleep. She said she had a headache and went off early. I've been asleep myself. I woke up and thought I heard a noise from her room, so I crept in to see if she was all right and found her gone. Her bed hadn't even been slept in. Then I checked on the boys. They'd gone too.' Her mouth dropped open as she caught sight of Tom and Joseph, who were climbing out of the jeep. 'Oh, my heavens! You're safe! But where's Afra? What's got into you kids?'

'We weren't with Afra. We don't know where she is. We went to look for her,' mumbled Tom. The electric currents of shock and anger vibrating in the atmosphere were making him nervous.

'Tidey, how could you be so grotesquely irres-ponsible?' Prof, unable to keep still, was striding up and down on his long legs outside the house. 'First you let Kamande go off with the Land Rover—'

'Julius is extremely sick,' said Aunt Tidey in a trembling voice. 'I suppose you think I should simply have let him die.'

Prof wasn't listening.

'You allow Afra to run off into the night,' he went on inexorably, 'and these boys to follow her. Don't you realize how incredibly dangerous it is out there?'

'*I* let them run off? It's my fault, is it?'

It was Aunt Tidey's turn to be angry now.

'That's so like you, Richard. Everyone else is always to blame, but never you. It's my fault, Kamande's fault, Afra's fault, is it? Well, let me tell you something. That poor child was distraught when you casually told her you weren't coming on her birthday outing. Have you no idea at all how much it meant to her? Do you realize what it does to a child when you break a promise?'

'Don't lecture me,' said Prof, who had stopped walking about and was standing still, frowning at his sister. 'I just want to find my daughter. I can do without a full character assessment right now.'

'I have to lecture you.' Aunt Tidey's large form was trembling with fury. 'I have to make you see. Look, Richard, I don't want to fight. We had a stupid quarrel twelve years ago. I came all this way to make it up, not to start over. We're family. We're all the family we have. We need each other and Afra needs you, only you're too blind to see it. You're cold and heartless and all closed up, and it's your fault she's run away. You have to be told. I can't just stand by and see you drive that little girl to despair.'

Prof put out his hands as if to fend her off.

'You've said enough,' he said stiffly. 'We can talk about who's to blame later. Now where is she? However are we going to find her?'

'We think she went back to the baboon rocks,'

Joseph said. 'She was very upset about the little baboon. He was hurt and he had been abandoned by his parents. She wanted to help him.'

There was a short silence. Prof swallowed.

'I see,' he said.

'She wanted Kamande to stop the car and go back to it after we left the picnic place,' Tom chipped in. 'She was really upset when he wouldn't.'

'So you think she went back up to the rocks, do you?' Prof was already turning back to the jeep. 'Are you sure of that?'

'No,' said Joseph, 'we can't be sure, but that's what we think.'

Aunt Tidey nodded.

'It's the most likely explanation,' she said.

Prof had jumped back into the jeep.

'I'm going to look for her,' he said.

'But you don't know the place,' said Aunt Tidey.

'Yes I do. I know this place well. We did an archaeological survey here one summer.'

He turned on the engine.

'Wait!' said Aunt Tidey, gathering up her robe. 'I'm coming with you.'

Prof put the jeep into gear.

'No, Tidey. Stay here. She may come back and she'll need you if she does. Anyway, I have to do this on my own.'

15

MEETING IN THE NIGHT

It was cold in the tree. A cutting wind whipped through the leaves, making them rattle. Afra drew her legs up cautiously to her chest, afraid she would fall, but the branch was wide enough to make a good platform. She could even let go with her hands and cross her arms, massaging herself to keep warm.

She was angry.

One father and one aunt, she thought. That's it. My entire family. That's all there is, and they might as well not be there at all. Prof doesn't even know I exist. He looks at me like he's never even seen me before. 'Oh! Here's a child! It walks and talks. Oh my! It takes up too much of my precious time. Goodbye, child.' And he's supposed to be my father, my *father*, for heaven's sake.

A mosquito whined round her head. She slapped at it and had to make a grab at the branch to regain her balance.

Why do I bother? she thought, listening out for the mosquito again. Why don't I just let it bite me, and I'd get malaria and not tell anyone so it was too late for medicine, and then I'd die. Who'd care? Who – would – care?

The memory of Aunt Tidey's hand on her shoulder by the campfire returned for a minute but she shrugged it off.

If she'd been the smallest little bit interested in me she wouldn't have stayed out of my life for twelve years. She'd have come over to visit before. It wasn't me she quarrelled with, after all. She couldn't have done. I was only just born.

She waggled her head and put on her aunt's New England accent. ' "Oh, Afra's just a baby, she doesn't account for much. Kids don't account for anything. Who cares about kids?" Anyway I'm still a baby to her. "Here's your birthday present, Afra honey. The cute little teeny-weeny kiddies' book of nature study. *Mrs Elephant sure loves her new little baby girl.*" Well, good for Mrs Elephant. It's more than some people do around here.'

From the rocks above came a barking sound. The baboons were stirring again.

'Babies do matter,' she whispered. 'You matter, baby. I'm staying here till I know you're OK.'

She looked back towards where the fire had been. She'd watched its faint glow while she'd been eating the last of her biscuits but she couldn't see it now. It had been good having it there, a little reminder of warmth and humanity in this vast, frightening, empty place. Now, seeing that it had gone, her anger ebbed away and she began to feel desolate.

If nobody loves you, what's the point of anything? she thought. You can love them till you burst but if they don't even notice you, don't ever think of you for five minutes together, why should you bother?

She was crying again, thick salt tears running down her cheeks.

'It's such a waste,' she muttered aloud. 'Such a waste! He just locks himself up, remembering *her*, and he's only got to turn round and see me. I must be a bit like her. She was my mother, after all. Why can't I take her place? I could do things for him, go off on his digs with him and look after his things, help him with his cataloguing like the students do, just be around when he wants someone to talk to.'

She fished the damp tissue out of her sleeve and wiped her nose with it again.

'It was all going to start this weekend. On my birthday. My new life with Prof. Well, that's just too bad, Afra. You're stuck with the old life, after all.'

Her foot was starting to cramp up. She stretched it out and rubbed it with her hands. She thought of the baboons, holding and grooming and reassuring each other up on the cold windswept rock.

I wish I was one of you, she thought. I wish I was anyone but me.

Then she remembered how they'd stared at her, how the one who'd seen her first had run about barking and warning all the others.

They don't want me either, she thought miserably. Only the baby might. He might really need me only he just doesn't know it yet.

She looked back up to the rocks.

'If only I could see you,' she whispered. 'If only I knew they were being nice to you.'

From far away in the distance came the rising calls of excited hyenas again. Afra shivered.

They've made their kill, she thought.

She listened intently, aware, now that the wind had dropped and the leaves were still, of other sounds, a snuffling that might be a porcupine, the faint rustling of a mouse or lizard in the dead leaves below the tree, the chucker-chucker of a nightjar.

Then, through the noises of the night, her sharp ears caught a new sound. It was the rumble of an engine.

They found out I've gone! she thought. Kamande's coming!

She imagined the Land Rover stopping beneath the tree just where it had been during the picnic. The lights would pick her up as it came up the hill. Kamande would see her at once.

'They won't get me! They mustn't!' she whispered.

She couldn't bear the idea of being dragged ignominiously back to the house, of being scolded and shouted at, of being patronized with silly promises to come back in the daylight.

I must hide! she thought frantically.

She swung herself down off the big branch and felt for the foothold with her dangling feet. She couldn't find it. The car was approaching fast. She could hear it change gear as it came up from the dip where the road divided. Panic seized her. She let go of the branch and crashed down onto the ground. A sharp pain stabbed through her ankle, but she got to her feet and hobbled along the hillside, away from the rocks. Kamande would look for her by the hollow where the baboon baby had been, she knew he would, but she'd hide further down, among the tumbled boulders below the crest of the ridge. He'd be unlikely to look for her there.

She reached the boulders just as the car pulled up. It had stopped some way below the tree. She heard the engine die away, the door open and slam shut, and hasty footsteps begin to run up the hill.

'Afra!' someone called. 'Afra, where are you!'

She was limping round behind the boulders, looking for a good place to hide when she heard him. She froze. It wasn't Kamande's voice.

Prof! It's Prof! He came after all! He's come for me! thought Afra. Her heart leapt with joy.

She was about to call out and run to him when he shouted again.

'Afra, stop all this nonsense. Come here!'

The anger in his voice chilled her and then her own anger rushed to meet his. She sat down on a boulder and folded her arms.

'Find me then,' she whispered. 'Go on, find me.'

She saw the beam of his torch jerk about as he shone it across the hillside. It passed right over her once but didn't falter.

He can't even pick me out from a pile of rocks, she thought savagely.

'Afra!' There was a desperate note in Prof's voice now. The torch flickered erratically over the hillside and Afra flinched as it shone straight into her face. The movement caught Prof's eye and he steadied the beam onto her.

'Afra!'

He was bounding across the hillside towards her now, shouting as he came. 'What do you think you're doing? Are you out of your mind? Are you trying to punish me or something, because you certainly succeeded.'

She stood up. She was trembling all over.

'Go away!' she tried to shout back, but her voice came out in a squeaking sob. 'I didn't ask you to come out here. Leave me alone.'

He had reached her now. The torch hung down from his hand and the beam hit the ground as they stared at each other face to face in the moonlight. Afra could see the anger die out of his eyes. He seemed to crumple.

'Oh sweetheart,' he said. 'I thought I'd lost you.'

He opened his arms and caught her up in them, swinging her into an embrace that was so tight it was almost painful. She could feel him shaking.

'Afra, I'm sorry,' he said. 'I'm so sorry.'

He's crying, she thought, astonished. He's actually crying.

'Don't, Daddy,' she said, her anger melting away. 'It's OK.'

She felt him drop a kiss onto her soft curly hair, then he set her down on her feet again.

'Come on,' he said, taking her hand. 'I'm taking you home.'

She went a couple of steps with him then pulled back.

'No. I have to stay here.'

He stopped and looked down at her.

'Why? Is it the baboon baby? Joseph said something about it. But, sweetheart, you can't take on a baboon.'

She pulled her hand away.

'I might have to. It might be my responsibility.'

He seemed about to say something but stopped himself.

'What do you want to do?'

'Stay here. Wait till dawn. See if his mother's taken him back. See if he's all right.'

She waited, expecting him to argue, to coax and scold her back to the car with him. Instead he said, 'Sure. We'll wait till dawn. I'll wait with you. But we'd be more comfortable in the car.'

She took his hand eagerly and squeezed it.

'Really? You'll really stay here with me? All night?'

In the moonlight she saw a smile pull up one corner of his mouth.

'Your aunt'll eat me alive. She'll have lost twenty pounds by dawn simply by fretting.'

'She's dumb.' Afra leaned her head on his arm. 'She's not like you at all.'

'Oh, she's not dumb. Don't be fooled by all her fussing. Tidey's one of the smartest people I know.'

They were walking together now, back towards the jeep, Afra limping on her painful ankle.

'She is?' Afra looked up at him. 'But you don't get along with her, do you?'

'We did once. We were close once.'

'What happened? Why did you quarrel?'

Prof didn't answer for a moment. Afra held her breath, afraid that she'd gone too far and that he'd pull back from her again.

'We quarrelled over you,' he said. 'When you were born, and your mother died, Tidey wanted to adopt you. To bring you up in America. She said I was crazy, bringing a child here on my own to Africa, that I'd never be able to give you everything you needed. She said such things . . .' He paused. 'I guess she was right after all.'

'No she wasn't!' Afra's ankle was hurting badly and she was finding it hard to keep up with him. 'I'd much rather have been with you. I only ever wanted to be with you.'

'You're so generous, sweetheart,' he said. 'Loyal and generous.'

He noticed for the first time that she was limping.

'What happened to your foot?'

'I had to climb a tree to get away from the hyenas,' she said matter-of-factly. 'Then when I heard a car coming I thought it was Kamande and he'd force me to go home. I wanted to run off and hide but I sort of fell while I was trying to climb down and twisted my ankle.'

'Oh baby,' he said. 'You must have been so lonely and frightened.'

He bent down and with one sweep of his arms picked her up. She snuggled her head into his shoulder. He hadn't carried her like that for years, not since she'd been a very little girl, when he used to come in at bedtime sometimes and sing her to sleep in his arms.

They reached the jeep and he slid her into the front seat, then took off her shoe and sock to look at her ankle. He bent it gently from side to side, looking up into her face. She tried to stifle her cry of pain.

'Brave, too,' he said. 'Like your mother. Just like your mother.'

'Tell me about her,' she whispered.

He put her shoe and sock back on.

'You haven't broken it,' he said. 'It's just a little sprain. It'll be better soon.'

She waited. He walked round to the far side of the jeep and climbed into the driver's seat. The moon, which was setting now, shone directly through the windscreen onto both their faces.

'What do you want to know?' he said.

'I killed her, didn't I?' said Afra. 'By being born. It was my fault she died.'

'No! You mustn't think that! It wasn't like that!' He put his arm round her and drew her close to lean on him. 'There was a civil war in Ethiopia before you were born,' he said, 'and a terrible famine. She came through it all but she'd lost many members of her family. Terrible things happened to her. She'd been hungry sometimes and had to run for her life, and she'd been . . . Oh, too many sad things had happened to her. Somewhere along the way damage had been caused to her heart.'

He had taken off his glasses and put them behind the steering wheel. He wiped his hand across his eyes.

'She wanted a baby. She wanted you more than anything else in the world. "This is going to be the first of many," she used to say. "We'll have a whole tribe of them to make up for all my lost family. An Ethiopian-American football team, Richard, half boys, half girls! What do you think of that?" She used to make me put my hand on her stomach to feel you kicking. "This one's trying to score goals already. She's something special. I know she is." ' His voice shook. 'Those nine months when she was carrying you were the happiest of her life. And of mine, too.' He stopped.

'It's OK, Daddy,' said Afra. 'You don't have to go on.'

He squeezed her shoulders.

'Tidey and I got her the best doctors we could afford,' he said. 'They were confident it would be OK, but when the moment came . . . it wasn't. You didn't kill her, sweetheart. Don't ever think that. That's the burden I bear. If she hadn't married me—'

'What? You mean you blame yourself?' Afra sat up. 'Prof, that's ridiculous. I never heard anything so dumb. She wanted to have a baby. She *wanted* me, you said so. I was her decision.'

'I wanted you too, don't forget.'

He pressed her nose with his forefinger and laughed.

'If you could only see yourself! You look like an indignant little monkey. Like this little baboon

of yours. Where are we going to keep him? Sarah's
not going to like it much.'

'We might not have to keep him,' Afra said
seriously. 'He might be all right.'

'Tell me about him,' said Prof. 'Tell me everything that happened.'

She sank back against his shoulder and began
to talk, and as she did she felt her heart expanding
with happiness in her chest until she was almost
afraid it would burst.

16

DAWN ON BABOON ROCK

The moon set soon after. Prof was asleep by then, his head with its shock of greying hair leaning back against the door of the jeep. He snored gently. For a while Afra watched the stars, a glorious mosaic of silver on black circling with infinite slowness overhead, then her eyelids drooped too and she slept, leaning against him for warmth, feeling safe within the shelter of the jeep.

She woke with a start as a bird, first herald of the dawn, landed on the roof, scratching the metal with its sharp claws. It took off again almost at once and flapped to the top of a nearby tree, breaking out into energetic song.

On the horizon, a strip of orange light was deepening and brightening minute by minute. Afra sat up. Light was stealing over the land. The black darkness had already softened to grey, and the grey was slowly warming into the pinky-red of the earth, and the green of the tree trunks, and the soft golden colour of the rocks.

Gently, not wishing to wake her father, she opened the door of the jeep and slid out. The baboons might be awake already. They might be moving off soon. She didn't want to miss the chance of seeing if the baby was safe with his mother again.

She took her first few steps gingerly, afraid that her ankle would hurt, but although she could still feel it, it wasn't too bad, and she set off cautiously up the hillside, not wanting to alarm them. The sun had just risen above the tilting earth and she could feel its rays warm on her back. The baboons had woken and were moving slowly off the rocks.

A big male had come down first. He had taken up his position on a chair-sized boulder near the hollow where the baby had been the day before. Other, younger males were coming up to greet him. He allowed some of the infants to groom him for a moment or two, then stood up and moved slowly, with a dignified gait, towards a female who was holding a baby in her arms.

It's him! My baby! I'm sure it's him! thought Afra, with a lurch of her heart.

The baby seemed a little listless. He lay on his side, his head against his mother's arm. The big male stopped beside them and reached for the baby, wanting to greet him, but the mother resisted him. The male, trying a new tack, began to gently groom her, working his searching fingers down her soft furry shoulder. Perhaps she would let him touch the baby soon.

A young female, who had been playing chase

with another small baboon, scampered up to them, leaping from boulder to boulder with sure, confident bounds. She touched the baby's head, as if to attract his attention. He winced and yelped, and turned to bare his little teeth at her.

'Yes, it's him,' whispered Afra.

She heard feet crunch on the stony ground behind her and turned round. Prof stood there.

'Is that the baby?' he said, looking across at the baby. 'That little guy?'

'Yes,' whispered Afra.

'Seems like he found his mom after all.'

'I guess so.'

They stood together for a while, watching the baboons in silence, then one by one the troop began to move, spreading out as they ambled peacefully across the countryside, pausing to pick and eat a flower or pounce excitedly on a fat grasshopper.

'Ready to go?' said Prof, looking down at Afra.

She gave a great sigh.

'Yes,' she said. 'I am.'

The jeep's engine was cold and wouldn't start at the first try. Prof turned the key twice while Afra looked round to see how far the baboons had gone. She saw something blue and white flapping against a bush halfway up the hill.

She chuckled.

'Wait a minute,' she said. 'I have to get something.'

She jumped out of the jeep, ran up to the bush and disentangled the tablecloth from the thorns.

'Don't I recognize that thing?' said Prof as she climbed back in beside him. 'It looks like our old tablecloth. How on earth did it get here?'

'Well, it's a long story,' said Afra happily. 'We had this picnic here yesterday, and—'

'Oh yes,' interrupted Prof. 'Tidey's famous cake. Was it good? Don't tell me. I can guess.'

'She put chilli in it instead of cinnamon,' said Afra. 'Kamande ate a whole piece. The boys ate theirs too and didn't even realize anything was wrong.'

'No!' said Prof, awestruck. 'I should have warned you about Tidey's cooking. She's a legend in her own time. But chilli in a birthday cake! That beats all!'

He put his head back and began to laugh. Afra started laughing too.

'It was an awful picnic,' she said. 'I didn't want to eat any of it anyway. I didn't want to leave the baby.'

He looked down at her.

'Are you disappointed?' he said. 'Did you really want to take him home?'

'Well . . . no, I guess not,' she said slowly. 'He's better with his own folks, I know that.'

It was funny, she thought, how feelings could change so fast. Yesterday she'd wanted nothing more than to hold the baby baboon in her arms,

155

to love and protect him and keep him with her for ever. Now, she wasn't sure why, she felt a little relieved that she wouldn't have to keep him after all. She was happy to think of him, safe with his mom, playing with his sister, being looked after until he grew strong again. It was right for him, she knew that.

Prof yawned.

'Oh boy,' he said. 'What a night. And what a dawn. I can't wait for breakfast. And a shower.'

Afra's thoughts were still far away. They'd jumped from the baboon's mother to her own.

'How did you meet her?' she said. 'My mother, I mean?'

He changed gear as he negotiated a sharp corner, shot a quick glance at her and looked back at the track.

'It was a bad time in Ethiopia,' he said. 'The worst. The civil war had been raging for years. Battles were being fought with heavy artillery up and down the country. A group of us – African archaeologists and historians mainly – were concerned about the ancient sites. We were afraid they were being destroyed. We set up a survey team to go into the country to see what could be done to protect them.'

Afra frowned.

'But what about the animals and the people? They're more important than a bunch of old stones. Wasn't it more important to protect them?'

He nodded slowly.

'I cared more about old stones than about people and animals in those days. Sablay taught me how wrong I'd been.'

'Go on,' said Afra, wriggling into a more comfortable position. 'What happened next?'

'We'd heard that some of the rock churches were being used as guerrilla hideouts. They were in danger of being shelled. Gems of ancient Ethiopian architecture! Some of the wonders of the world!'

'Go on, admit it,' said Afra smiling up at him. 'You still care about buildings more than people.'

He smiled ruefully.

'Maybe, but I'm working on it. Anyway, early one morning we set off on foot towards a church high up in the mountains. We'd heard gunfire in the night but it had died away in the distance. I turned a corner – it was a little mountain path, very steep, with a sheer drop on one side and the most incredible view – and there she was, your mother, sitting on a rock, looking as if the whole of Ethiopia was spread out at her feet. Her leg was wrapped in an old rag and blood was seeping through it. She'd been working with a relief team, trying to evacuate the wounded, and she'd been hit herself in the night. She was waiting for someone to pass by who would stop and help her down the track to find a doctor.'

'What did you do?' said Afra, who was hanging on his words.

'She didn't complain at all,' he went on, ignoring her question.

'Did you help her? Did you take her to a doctor?' said Afra.

'Yes. Our team split up. Half of us went on to find the church. I persuaded the others to turn back and help her down the path. She'd lost a lot of blood and was very weak but she was so brave. So brave . . . I knew by the time we'd got back down the mountain and were on our way to the emergency medical post that I wanted to marry her.'

Afra couldn't speak. She felt still and solemn. She wanted him to tell her the story again, to add more details, to paint a more vivid picture, but it was enough for now. She had plenty to think about now.

'Did you ever go back to that place again?'

'No.' He shook his head. 'The war swept through the whole area after that. No, I never went back.'

'I'd like to go there,' said Afra. 'One day.'

His hands tightened on the steering wheel.

'Yes,' he said. 'Yes. I'll take you there. One day we'll go there together.'

17

CATERPILLARS FOR BREAKFAST

As the jeep turned in through the gate and pulled up in front of the house, Prof and Afra could see Aunt Tidey standing on the verandah. She didn't move.

'Oh dear,' said Prof softly. 'This is going to be a tough one, baby. Are you ready for it, or shall we just turn round and run away?'

Afra giggled.

'She'd murder us.'

'Poor Tidey, we wouldn't give her the chance. We'd disappear for ever. On second thoughts, I guess we did that before. Twelve years is long enough. It's face the music time.'

He jumped out of the jeep. Afra followed him. Her ankle felt better now. She could hardly feel the pain at all.

'Tidey, listen,' Prof was saying, 'I'm sorry.'

Afra, looking round from behind him, saw that Aunt Tidey's eyes were puffy and red and that the rest of her face was pale.

'*You're* sorry?' she said. 'When I think of all the things I said to you, calling you cold and heartless ... but you're back! Afra's safe! That's all that matters.' She looked at Afra. 'Oh honey, you must have been so terribly unhappy. I couldn't bear to think of you running off like that, all alone, in the dark. I was scared I'd never see you alive again. I haven't slept all night. I felt I'd let you down so badly.'

Her cheeks were wet with tears.

Afra looked at her. Aunt Tidey didn't seem absurd or irritating any more. She looked kind and loving, dignified even, in spite of her messy hair and crumpled pink clothes.

'You didn't let me down,' Afra said. 'You tried to give me a good time but I guess I wouldn't let you.'

Tom and Joseph burst excitedly out of the door behind Aunt Tidey.

'Afra, you total maniac!' shouted Tom. 'What happened? Did you see our fire?'

'Was it your fire? Yes, I did. I thought it was nomads.'

'We lit it to show you the way home,' said Joseph.

'Thanks.' Afra grinned at them. 'It was great. It really made me feel good, just seeing it and knowing there were other human beings out there.'

'Weren't you scared, I mean terrified totally out of your mind?' said Tom, looking at her admiringly. 'I would have been. It was bad enough just going up the hill on our own, but the moon was out by then and there were two of us anyway. Did you find the little baboon?'

'Yes. He's OK. The troop did come back. I saw him this morning, with his mom.'

'Is Afra all right? She hasn't come to any harm?' Aunt Tidey was saying in a low voice to Prof. 'Just psychologically she could have been absolutely traumatized.'

'She's fine.' Prof put his arm round his sister's shoulders. 'Really fine. I found her quite easily but she didn't want to come back until she'd made sure the little baboon was OK. I knew you'd be out of your mind, worrying about her, but it was important to do this together. We had stuff to sort out.'

She nodded, but she was still overwrought.

'It was the elephants! I couldn't get them out of my mind.'

'What elephants?' Prof looked bewildered.

'They were around the house the night before last. I found fresh dung yesterday all over.'

'Here? Elephants here? Did they do any damage?'

'No.' She looked at him reproachfully. 'But they might have done. They might have attacked Afra, too.'

He laughed.

'Oh Tidey, I'll admit to everything. I'll agree that it's all been my fault from start to finish but you really can't blame me for the elephants. I didn't see any sign of them. If they were here, they must be over the hills and far away by now anyway. Listen, I'm starving. Can we have something to eat? Afra must be half dead with hunger too. From what she tells me she ate nothing at all yesterday.'

'Breakfast!' Aunt Tidey threw her hands up. 'Of course! Boys, get the fire started. I guess you two'll want showers.'

She hurried into the house. Afra followed her. She'd suddenly realized that she'd never been so hungry in her entire life. She couldn't wait for breakfast. She needed something to eat right now.

In the kitchen Aunt Tidey was leaning over the nesting box. The front of it was open and from the inside came a strange rasping noise. Afra looked over Aunt Tidey's shoulder.

'Meet Jonathan Swift,' said Aunt Tidey. 'He fell out of his nest again. There was no point in trying to put him back. I'm afraid we'll just have to take him home with us and look after him until he can fly.'

Afra looked at the little bird. He was funny and pathetic and indignant all at the same time. She took a deep breath.

'Right,' she said. 'You can leave him to me, Aunt Tidey. Rearing baby birds is something I know about.'

She looked critically at the nest Aunt Tidey had carefully constructed out of torn up kitchen paper.

It was a little too neat to be comfortable, but it would do for the moment. Without touching him, she tried to examine the side of his head and body. He looked unharmed. Afra nodded, satisfied. She'd have him up and on the wing in next to no time.

The baby swift sensed her presence. His enormous beak gaped open and he made his whirring, chirring demand for food.

Aunt Tidey, who had started fetching out the breakfast things, looked over her shoulder.

'He really is the greediest little thing I ever did see,' she said. 'I suppose he won't be satisfied unless he gets his breakfast first.'

She put down the loaf she was carrying and opened a matchbox that was sitting by the nesting box on the table. It was full of grubs and insects.

'I drop one into his beak every time I go past,' she said. 'You wouldn't believe how many he's eaten already.'

She made a face as she picked up a caterpillar.

'You have no idea, little Jonathan, how privileged you are,' she said severely. 'Nothing but the direst necessity would ever have persuaded me to handle bugs with my bare hands.'

She dropped the caterpillar into the gaping beak and smiled as the baby bird gulped it down.

'There you go, dear,' she said.

'Where did you find all these bugs?' said Afra.

'Oh honey, it is truly astonishing how many

there are in close proximity to the house. It took me only five minutes to collect this entire boxful. I went out looking as soon as it was light and found a shrub out there that is positively infested with them. Do you suppose it's possible to over-feed a baby swift?'

Afra laughed.

'I guess not. He'd just refuse to go on eating, wouldn't he? Like a baby human.'

'I really have no idea.' Aunt Tidey smiled indulgently down at Jonathan, whose beak was already wide open again. She fished another caterpillar out of the matchbox. 'I tried looking it up in . . . in your new nature book. It wasn't exactly informative on the subject of rearing baby birds. As a matter of fact, it was a little . . . well, juvenile, on most things. I'm sorry, honey. It's hard to pick out the right present when you don't know someone, and I didn't know you at all.'

'I didn't know you, either,' said Afra, smiling as Aunt Tidey tweaked the baby swift's paper nest a little to tidy it up. She suddenly wanted to put her arms round her aunt's soft, ample body and give her a hug.

Instead she said, 'There are some tweezers in the jeep, in the first-aid box. Why don't I get them? Then we wouldn't have to pick up all these creepy-crawlies in our fingers. Anyway, you're supposed to poke the food a little way down their gullets, like their parents do with their beaks. Otherwise he might choke.'

Aunt Tidey looked at her admiringly.

'What logical minds children have. Why didn't I think of tweezers and beaks myself? Uh-oh, Jon's hungry again already. Go get those tweezers now. Quite frankly, I've had enough of fishing around in that matchbox.'

Afra ran out to the jeep. She passed Prof, who was coming into the house.

'Is breakfast on the way?' he said. 'I can't wait much longer.'

'We haven't started fixing it yet,' said Afra. 'Aunt Tidey's sent me out to find some tweezers so we can pick up the caterpillars.'

A look of horror crossed Prof's face.

'Caterpillars?' he said. '*Caterpillars?* For breakfast? Has she taken leave of her senses?'

Afra gave a crack of laughter.

'Don't worry,' she said. 'They're for Jonathan Swift, not for us.'

Prof stared at her.

'Did you say Jonathan Swift?' he said. 'This place is a madhouse. There's nothing for it, I'll have to do the breakfast myself.'

He marched off towards the kitchen.

Outside, Tom and Joseph were busy building up the fire. Flames were crackling merrily round the huge water pot. Afra ran to the jeep, opened the first-aid box and found the tweezers. She was about to take them in to her aunt when she stopped. Singing was surging out through the kitchen window, a rich voice, high and clear, was pouring out the most wonderful music. A deeper voice joined it a moment later and the duet was so lovely that Afra, Tom and Joseph stood rooted to the spot, unable to move.

'I didn't know we had a radio here,' said Tom.

'We haven't,' said Joseph. 'It must be Aunt Tidey and Prof.'

'Can't be,' said Afra. 'I've never heard Prof sing like that. I've never heard him sing at all.'

They went up to the kitchen window and stood in a row looking in. Prof was beating up eggs in a big bowl. Aunt Tidey was slicing bread. They were both singing at the tops of their voices.

They caught sight of the three faces in the window, stopped singing and started laughing.

'Don't stop,' said Afra reverently. 'It was wonderful. I didn't know you could sing like that, Prof.'

Prof grinned.

'I'm not much good, but Tidey, she's the best. Nearly became an opera singer. Could have done if she'd wanted to.'

Aunt Tidey grimaced.

'No thank you. Think of the life. You can never call your soul your own. How's the water coming along, boys? Is it boiling yet?'

Afra went round through the front door and

into the kitchen. Jonathan Swift, encouraged by the singing, was doing some cheeping of his own. Afra picked up a grub in the tweezers and dropped it into his mouth.

'Are you sure this little bird's a swift, Aunt Tidey?' she said. 'He'll grow so fast with all this food, maybe he'll turn into an ostrich.'

Outside the house, the boys were still collecting wood for the fire.

'Hey,' said Tom, looking up. 'Isn't that a car I can hear? Kamande must be coming back.'

The Land Rover was in sight now, coming down the track towards the house.

'He will be so impressed by our fire,' said Joseph, leaning over to put another log on to it. 'It's *big*.'

'What's that?' said Tom. 'Something's just fallen out of your pocket. Look, down there, by that burning log.'

Joseph screwed up his eyes to look down into the heat, then gasped and jumped back.

'It's the unexploded cartridge!' he yelled. 'It'll explode! Quick, we must get it out!'

He grabbed a stick and poked at the fire, making the cartridge roll free.

'What were you boys shouting about?' said a voice behind them. Tom and Joseph jumped. Prof had come out of the house, with Aunt Tidey behind him.

'We . . . um . . .' began Tom, his voice dying away as Joseph dug him in the ribs.

Luckily, at that moment, Kamande pulled the Land Rover up beside them.

'You are here!' he said to Prof. 'That is good.'

Prof held the door open as Kamande jumped out.

'How's Julius?' he said. 'What happened?'

'He is sick,' said Kamande, 'but the doctor has given him medicine. I found his nephew who is staying with him now. He will be better soon, the doctor said.'

'Oh, that's such a relief,' said Aunt Tidey. 'That poor man. I've never seen such a fever on anyone. Hey, what's that smell?'

'My eggs!' shouted Prof. 'They're burning!'

'And you say *I* can't cook,' said Aunt Tidey, running after him.

It was the best breakfast Afra had ever had. They carried the big table outside and set it up under a tree, then sat out in the cool air of the morning and ate eggs and bacon and toast and pancakes while overhead starlings with iridescent blue feathers whistled and sang as if they were a band sent round to provide the music.

They got up from the table at last and began to clear away the dishes. Prof felt in his pocket.

'It's all very well for you young things,' he said, 'but it's too bright out here for me. My middle-aged eyes need sunglasses.'

He went into the house.

'And my middle-aged face needs sun lotion,' said Aunt Tidey. 'So do your young ones, I'm sure, but you won't thank me for telling you.'

Afra went up to her and hugged her.

'It was an amazing breakfast, Aunt Tidey,' she said, 'and the pancakes were hardly burnt at all. Not nearly as bad as Prof's eggs, anyway.'

Prof wandered outside again.

'Have any of you seen a small red spectacle case?' he said. 'I've been hunting for my sunglasses all over.'

Aunt Tidey started guiltily.

'Was that little red case yours?' she said. 'It was lying around on the table, so I—'

'Don't tell me. You tidied it away,' said Prof. 'Oh Tidey, you don't change, do you?'

Tidey looked at her brother shrewdly.

'I can't say the same for you,' she said. 'Something tells me you've changed considerably in a remarkably short space of time.'

Afra was so happy, she had the strange sensation that she might at any moment take off and float into the air.

'It's a funny thing,' she said. 'It was my worst birthday ever yesterday, but today's my best day-after-my-birthday ever.'

'Oh! That reminds me.' Prof felt in his pocket and pulled out a little box. 'I have something for you. Your birthday present.'

'You gave it to me already,' said Afra. 'You gave me some money, remember?'

'It's an extra present then,' said Prof. He put the box into Afra's hands. She opened it.

'Oh!' she gasped. 'It's perfect! It's beautiful!'

On a cushion of velvet lay a golden Ethiopian cross worked in the finest filigree. Attached to it was a long gold chain.

Afra picked it up, let the chain run through her fingers and held the cross up to the sun, so that the yellow metal sparkled in the light.

Behind her, she heard Aunt Tidey draw in her breath.

'Sablay's cross,' she said quietly.

'Yes,' said Prof. 'Sablay's cross for Sablay's daughter.'